NOTES
FROM A
COMA

Mike McCormack is an award-winning novelist and short story writer from Mayo. His previous work includes *Getting it in the Head* (1996) and *Forensic Songs* (2012). In 1996 he was awarded the Rooney Prize for Irish Literature for *Getting it in the Head* and in 2007 he was awarded a Civitella Ranieri Fellowship. In 2016, *Solar Bones* won the Goldsmiths Prize and the BGE Irish Book of the Year award.

Also by Mike McCormack

Getting it in the Head
Crowe's Requiem
Forensic Songs
Solar Bones

NOTES
FROM A
COMA

MIKE McCORMACK

CANONGATE

This Canons edition published in 2017 by Canongate Books Ltd,
14 High Street, Edinburgh EH1 1TE

First published in Great Britain by Jonathan Cape, London, 2005

www.canongate.co.uk

1

British Library Cataloguing-in-Publication Data
A catalogue record for this book is available on
request from the British Library

ISBN 978 1 78689 141 9

Printed and bound in Great Britain by Clays Ltd, St Ives plc.

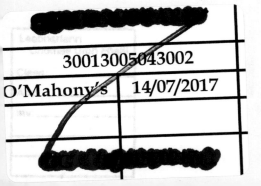

When my perceptions are removed for any time, as by sound sleep, so long am I insensible of myself, and may truly be said not to exist.

—David Hume

My guiding principle is this: Guilt is never to be doubted.

—Franz Kafka, *In the Penal Colony*

NOTES FROM A COMA[†]

Event Horizon

[†] . . . because he is now both stimulus and qualia. His name, blurting
through the nation's print and electronic media, is also one of those
synapses at which the nation's consciousness forms itself. Firing in
debate and opinion polls, across editorial maunderings and the
antiphonal call-and-response formats of radio phone-ins, his suspended
mind is one of those loci at which the nation's consciousness knows
itself and knows itself knowing itself . . .

His existence—it is not too strong a word—is now a continuous incident report. Each day, the newspaper of record carries an abstract of
his EEG tracings across a six-column spread inside the front page. All
over the country children above and below the age of reason chart the
peaks and troughs of his delta waves across the walls of their class-
rooms. Cast out over the earth's cortex also a continuous stream of his
MRI and EEG tracings. They have the appearance of meteorological
reports from another star—troughs and banks of high pressure, depres-
sions and tidal movements. Electronically flayed, these images are
drawn down to our bedrooms and workstations, pegged out to dry
across screens and monitors. Bootlegged already by the fashion and
design industry they are now protected by retroactive copyright and
patent legislation; the author has asserted his moral right . . .

He evokes a response and this is to our credit. Contrary to ongoing
analysis the nation's compassion reflex has not been habituated. There
is real concern, a genuine anxiety beyond the compassion flash fires
of the latest crisis de jour. He touches our soul and, in a happy con-
gruence of myth and politics, the public interest is now of interest to
the public. We are not entirely mindful of him but we do bear him
in mind . . .

1

FRANK LALLY

My heart went out to Anthony that day, that's no lie. Nearly twenty years ago now but I remember it like it was last week.

It was about two o'clock in the afternoon when the cars and the cattle truck came up the road. I followed them up and when I got to the yard the truck had reversed into the barn door and the vet and the bailiffs were already loading up the herd. Anthony was standing at the back of the house with the collar pulled up around his ears. I went over and stood beside him and said nothing. What could I say?[†]

A dirty day it was too, pissing rain all morning and a wind blowing through the yard that would shave you. No one said anything but it didn't take them more than twenty minutes to load up the whole herd—eight Friesian cows, a

---

[†] In January of that year one of the first cases of BSE in the republic broke out on the farm of Anthony O'Malley in Louisburgh, west Mayo.

After two days watching a Friesian cow with two permanent teeth stagger through the yard, unable to keep her balance and obviously disorientated, the beast was isolated and the vet summoned. Simon Conway's provisional diagnosis was for an incurable neurological disorder. The animal was destroyed, blood and brain tissue samples were taken—sealed, dated, numbered and referred to the national laboratories in Dublin for analysis. Six days later a case of BSE was confirmed and in accordance with control measures brought in the

couple of yearlings and two calves. One by one they marched up that ramp without a bit of bother and I remember thinking we'd often had more trouble loading up two or three beasts of a Monday morning for the mart.

They pinned up the tailgate and moved off and I saw the sergeant, Jimmy Nevin, coming over to Anthony. But whatever was on his mind he thought better of it and stood off holding the gate for the truck. Anthony turned into the house without a word. I watched the truck down the bottom of the hill and saw it turn out on to the main road. Jimmy Nevin closed the gate and walked over to me.

"Before you go," he said, "give him this."

He handed me a brown envelope.

"It's the quarantine order. Six months."

Anthony got barred from Thornton's that night and it was years afterwards before he could have a drink in it.

There was a time when Anthony had a reputation for being able to start a fight in an empty room: a short temper and tidy with his fists. I'd seen him in action a few times, London and elsewhere, and he wasn't a man you wanted to do battle with. But that was all in the past—or so I thought. It all came back to him that night in Thornton's.

---

previous year Anthony O'Malley's entire herd was taken away to be destroyed.

The destruction of entire herds containing infected animals would only become compulsory nine years later in the UK and other EU countries. Coming on the back of agreed measures drawn up in the Florence Agreement, it represented a further expansion of the offspring cull, a measure referred to unofficially as the Herod Option.

He'd been drinking since mid-afternoon and by eleven he was well on it. Ger, behind the bar—he was only young at the time—wouldn't serve him any more. He came outside the bar and tried to lead Anthony to the door. Anthony of course was having none of it. He'd come in under his own steam, he'd go out the same way. And he did too a few minutes later when he saw he was getting no more drink. But that wasn't the end of it. You'd want to get Eileen Flynn to tell you this story, she was there that night and she has a better telling of it than I have. She laughed about it afterwards but she was lucky she wasn't killed the same night. Bang! The big window inside the door bursts in and this yellow gas bottle hops off her table and skids along the floor to the counter. Anthony is outside in the pissing rain, the sleeves of his shirt rolled up and the jacket down beside him in the channel. Any man, he was roaring, any fucking man!

He spent that night in the barracks and he was lucky he didn't spend a lot longer. Thornton's didn't press charges. They knew the craic and they settled for the price of a table and a new window but they told Anthony he'd have to do his drinking somewhere else. I got a call from Jimmy Nevin the next morning and went down to the barracks to bring him home. Of course by then the whole town was talking about him. Driving home with him that day I never thought that three months down the road he'd be giving them a whole lot more to talk about. That's when he docked up with JJ.

ANTHONY O'MALLEY

Not a day's gone by, not an hour, when I don't think of him lying out there on that ship in the Killary.[†] And the thing that comes back to me are all the arguments we used to have. How he'd sit there where you're sitting now, in that very chair, covered in diesel and cement after his day's work. More likely than not he'd have a few pints on him, probably drinking since after work. And it'd always begin the same way.

"A consumer durable, Anthony, wasn't that how it was?"

"Go to bed, JJ. Have you eaten?"

"Never mind eating, tell me the story. The bargaining process, tell me that again."

I'd make him something to eat then, a sandwich or a bowl of soup, because likely as not he'd have nothing

---

[†] A child's geography book will tell you that the Killary is the only proper fjord on the Irish coastline. Running six kilometres west–east through Ordovician sandstone and Silurian quartzite it forms part of the Mayo–Galway border. At one time its steep sides and sheltered waters called out for mineral prospecting, cheap holiday accommodation, mussel farming and marine leisure activities. Now hemmed in by protective legislation, it is the focal feature of an extensive national park and is marked down in tourist guides for sightseers travelling in this part of the world.

What no tourist bumf will tell you is that this inlet is suffused with

solid in his stomach since dinner time. But he'd have no interest in food. All he wanted to hear was the story, his story.

"Two thousand dollars, wasn't that it?"

"Eat up, JJ, it's past midnight."

"That was the going rate at the time, wasn't it? Over three thousand Deutschmarks or eleven hundred pounds if you could find someone to take sterling?"

It could go on all night. He could sit there teasing out every detail of it, hearing it for the umpteenth time and still, after all these years, bewildered by it.

"And what was the asking price, Anthony, what was the reserve? Was it stamped across my forehead or was there a little tag dangling from my toe?"

"It wasn't like that."

"So what was your opening bid? I'd say you came in low—low and hard. You wouldn't want to show your hand too early. Eight hundred pounds, was that it? Not much more surely?"

"Go to bed, JJ, this isn't the time."

---

an atmosphere of ineffable sadness. Partly a trick of the light and climatic factors, partly also the lingering residue of an historical tragedy which still resonates through rock and water down seven generations of fretful commemorative attempts and dissonant historical hermeneutics. Now think of grey shading towards gunmetal across an achromatic spectrum; think also of turbid cumulus clouds pouring down five centimetres of rainfall above the national average and you have some idea of the light reflected within the walls of this inlet. This is the type of light which lends itself to vitamin D deficiency, baseline serotonin levels, spluttering neurotransmitters and mild but by no means notional depression. It is the type of light wherein ghosts go their rounds at all hours of the day.

"Did you spit on your hand to seal the deal, like a proper cattle jobber."

"It wasn't like that and you know it."

"Of course it wasn't like that but it's the truth, isn't it? And a seller's market too, wasn't it? They couldn't keep up with demand. All of us there up on top of one another in our slatted house."

"It wasn't a slatted house, JJ, it was an orphanage. Christ, you know all this, I've told you a hundred times. Why do you have to keep going over it?"

"It's a story, Anthony, a bedtime story. Tell me about the wicked witch. We wouldn't want to forget her. Tell me again about the wicked witch."

I'd go along with him from here. He'd be so far into it the best thing was to get through it as quickly as possible and try to get to bed.

"Her name was Dragana, wasn't that it?"

"Yes, JJ, her name was Dragana."

"And she had a pair of arms on her like a butcher and a hooked nose with a wart on it. Her broomstick stood in the corner."

"Whatever you say, JJ."

This was where he'd start laughing, leaning forward in his chair, his favourite part.

"But you took no shite from her, isn't that right?"

"That's right, JJ, I put manners on her."

"Witch or no witch you let her know who's boss."

"Yes, JJ, I sorted her."

"You haggled with her, wasn't that what you did?"

"Yes, JJ, I haggled with her."

7

He'd be bent over laughing now, laughing or crying I could never tell from the tears rolling down his cheeks.

"Haggled with her," he'd gasp, nearly choking. "This is the bit that kills me. You actually haggled her down to two thousand dollars." The mug of tea or soup would be slopping down the side of the chair. "The going rate for a healthy child was two and a half thousand dollars but you haggled her down to two thousand."

"Yes, JJ, I haggled her."

"And shook hands on two thousand."

"Yes."

Some nights it might end here, the worst of it over, but most nights he'd want to take it through to the bitter end.

"It could have been a lot worse though, couldn't it? You could have used the old barter system."

"Yes, JJ, something."

"No, not just something. Tell the story right, don't be trying to get away from it. Cigarettes and televisions, those were the things, weren't they? Explain the cigarettes to me again."

There was no way out now—I'd have to see it through to the end.

"The place was in turmoil, JJ, the economy was a shambles and the currency was virtually worthless. The gold standard was a packet of cigarettes. A packet of Kent cigarettes traded at two dollars."

"So you could have had me for a thousand packs of cigarettes."

"If you want to put it that way."

8

"I don't want to put it that way but that's the way it was, wasn't it?"

This was where he'd sink back in his chair with that look on his face. This was where he'd start talking to himself.

"And no one thought it was strange. No one said stall the ball, this isn't right. You can't put your hand down in your hip pocket and hand over a wad of notes for a child. That day is gone. No one saw anything wrong with it?"

"You don't know what it was like. The chaos, the violence, the conditions in those orphanages. You were lucky, JJ."

I remember the first time I said that to him, the look on his face. Like I'd scalded him or struck him with the back of my hand. I thought he was going to hit me. But he just slumped back in his chair and looked into his mug.

"I'm going to bed, JJ. You have to be up for work."

"I'll have a last fag, I'll go then. Goodnight."

"Don't stay up all night."

But of course he would. I'd find him in the morning slumped back on that chair you're in now with an ashtray of butts on the floor beside him. He'd have stayed up all night smoking and mulling things over. About him being lucky and the haggling and about what he called his life as a consumer durable.

He looked anything but durable the first time I saw him. Lying in a crib he was with six others, them all up on top of one another like a litter of bonamhs only not half as clean. Like the rest of them he was scalded in his own water and looking out between the bars of the crib with the biggest pair of eyes you've ever seen on a child. They were that big I thought they'd jump out of his head and roll across the floor to my feet. And if there was any colour to them I couldn't tell what it was from the bad light in the room. Black as coal they were and probably just as hard, I remember thinking. But that was just a trick of the light. I now know JJ's eyes are a kind of deep ruby red, the colour of strong tea without milk. It's not the type of colour that shows itself. You have to look hard to find it.

Standing there looking at him I thought the room was full of wasps; there was this buzzing noise everywhere. But it couldn't be wasps. This was the middle of March, there was eight inches of snow outside on the ground—not even that demented city could have wasps and snow at the same time. And then I knew. They were grinding their teeth. The kids, every one of them, grinding their teeth down to the gums and making this buzzing noise that was filling the room. Sitting on their behinds, sprawled across each other, lying on their backs, every one of them working their jaws from side to side, chewing nothing but cold fresh air.†

So there I was pacing the room with my hands clasped

---

† In December of the previous year the Conducator stood on the balcony of the Central Committee building in Palace Square and addressed the crowd below. His voice, carrying in the sub-zero temperature to the back of the square, assured the crowd that the great collective experiment of the last three decades was in no way compromised by recent political developments in neighbouring countries.

As always on such occasions his wife stood shoulder to shoulder with him. Through four decades this has been her place—it has indeed been a great love affair. They have drawn strength from each other

behind my back, trying to look like I knew what I was doing, peering into the cribs like a cattle jobber looking at weanlings. But what did I know about finding a child—a forty-three-year-old bachelor from the west of Ireland with neither niece nor nephew? I hadn't a clue where to start looking . . .

I took a few more turns round the room peering into the other cribs, not wanting to rush things nor give anything away. At the back of the room, just inside the door, there stood a woman with her arms folded across her chest like a bouncer. JJ calls her Dragana but I can never remember hearing her name. Like the hooked nose and the broomstick it was one of those details he made up. But he was right about the arms. She was built like a wrestler, her coat looked like it was going to come apart at the shoulders. This was a woman you didn't want to mess with. This was her orphanage and these were her kids. If any of them were leaving the room it would only be through her. She was the one who would fix up the paperwork and exit visas. She was the one who would take a percentage of whatever money changed hands.

I didn't want her forcing my hand so I just kept walking

---

and they have needed every bit of it; together they have destroyed an entire country. Bearing in mind that the country was one of God's masterpieces to begin with this is no small feat . . .

Eight minutes into the rally the crowd gets restless, a definite low-level hum begins to undercut the autarch's speech. At first nothing more than a rustle but already it is the authentic sound of dissent, a sound without precedent in the annals of such occasions. It builds slowly, now clearly audible, strengthening under its own strength, three decades of shame and privation surfacing. The Conducator's face twitches in disbelief, a fleeting shadow crossing the blankness of his cheekbones. His wife leans into him and quite audibly says, "Promise

round the room. But those eyes kept turning me round and drawing me back to that little face pressed between the bars. He was wearing these big pyjamas with the leg ends frayed from dragging through the dampness and filth in the bottom of the crib. And if there was any colour or pattern on them under that filth I couldn't make it out. But there was this look on his face, a look I've never seen on any child or adult before or since. It was like he was saying to me, "I'm the child you've come for, forget the rest. I'm the one you've come for." He wasn't saying he was any better or stronger or healthier than any of the others. All he was saying was that he was the one. And he was right; he was the one I had come for. I could have gone round that room a hundred times and looked in a thousand other cribs throughout the city and I knew I would have ended up back at that same spot looking down at that child with those black eyes and those filthy pyjamas. This was my child, big eyes, white knuckles and everything. We just stared at each other and there might as well have been just the two of us in that room. If there was a

---

them something. Talk to them." This is the precise moment when history fractures, the point at which a specific time has run its course. This moment separates before from after. A new epoch has begun, a new calendar starts from this moment.

Four days from this, on Christmas Day, the Conducator and his wife will sit in a child's school desk in a military barracks arraigned before a hastily convened court. The charges against them will range from corruption and impoverishment of a nation to mass murder. Recording proceedings against God knows what sort of reprisals the video footage will show that as the charges are being read out the Conducator gazes at his watch like a man concerned with missing an

specific moment when our lives came together this was it. Something clicked between us. I felt like putting my hand out and introducing myself, saying, hello, my name is Anthony O'Malley from Louisburgh in the west of Ireland. You probably haven't heard of the place but in a few days when everything is sorted I'm taking you out of here and you and me are going to have a long and happy life together. But of course I didn't. Things were strange enough without me talking to a child who couldn't understand one word I was saying. And then for one moment I had the feeling there was something wrong with him. He was sitting stock-still, not the tiniest movement out of him. For some reason I thought there might be something wrong with his head, his sight or his hearing or something. But it wasn't that. I waved my hand in front of his face and his eyes followed it over and back. I shouted softly beside his ear and he started sideways. But there was still this stillness about him . . . The boss woman, Dragana, came up behind me and began telling me something. I didn't hear her. It had dawned on me why he was so still; he was the only one in the crib not grinding his teeth.

The boss woman was pulling on my sleeve and talking

---

important engagement elsewhere. It will be a moment of studied, elegant contempt. Refusing a plea of mental instability he will hold his nerve and say that he refuses to recognise the court and will answer only to the Grand National Assembly; an old hand at this sort of thing himself he will recognise a show trial when he sees one. When the death sentence is read out and as he is being led from the room we will hear him humming "The Internationale." His wife, however, in a last outburst will brush aside a young soldier who reaches to assist her. Her last recorded words will be, "Take your hands off me, motherfucker."

away. She was telling me something, the child's name, I think. But she didn't have to tell me. I knew his name, I'd known it from the moment I'd first set eyes on him. His name was John Joe O'Malley and I was going to call him JJ.

It took four days to round up the paperwork: medical certs, exit visa and so on. They were the longest four days of my life. At first I thought it would be a simple job of handing over the money and walking out of there with him in my arms and getting a plane home. That's how much I knew.

Now that I had chosen JJ I itched to get out of that city. I wanted to take him away from that orphanage, away from the filth and the dampness and the paint peeling off the walls and the smell of detergent that would choke you. I was so worried someone might come and lift him out from under my nose that I spent every minute of those four days standing over him and talking to him, just getting used to him. When I saw him a couple of days later he'd been taken from his crib and was sitting by himself in a separate cot at the back of the room. He was wearing a new pair of pyjamas and there were clean sheets under him. For the first time I had a clear view of him and I hardly recognised him with all the dirt stripped off him. His eyes were still dark but his skin was several shades lighter and I knew straight away that this was one thing that would set him apart when I got him home. Of course what I couldn't see then were all the other things that would make life so awkward for him, all the grief and misery which has him lying out there today on that ship with pipes draining and feeding him.[†] All I saw that day was a little boy who needed love and attention, a thin hardy boy with eyes round from hunger, eyes balanced over those high cheekbones like two marbles.

We got back to Ireland on the twenty-second of March, flew into Shannon at two o'clock in the afternoon and I was never so happy to see rain in all my life. One hundred and fifty pounds it cost to get a taxi from Shannon to the door here, 130 miles the driver told me. It was half six when I brought JJ O'Malley through the back door of the old house and he must have felt right at home the minute he got inside. You have to remember this is the old house I'm talking about—bad roof and damp walls and draughts coming in under the doors rattling the window frames. I stood there in the middle of the floor with him in my arms watching our breath cloud up in front of us and it was as cold as a grave.

We were in about an hour, the fire down and me feeding him a bowl of soup on my knee when the knock came to the door. I knew before it swung open who it was; he'd have seen the light in the window.

"Frank," I called, without getting up, "come in."

He was in the middle of the floor before he noticed JJ.

[†] Registered to Interskan Shipping out of Antwerp, *Le Soleil Noir*, an eighty-metre cargo coaster, had for ten years plied its trade ferrying alumina trihydrate to the municipal water systems of coastal cities in the North Sea and Baltic. Detained by Dutch immigration authorities when a backload of pig iron from the Russian Federation was found to be bulked out with twenty refugees from Kaliningrad, the vessel had lain in Antwerp pending the trial of its owner, Hans Luyxx.

You could see him nearly take a step backwards. I never let on.

"Take a seat, Frank," I said. "Push out the door."

Frank swung a chair out from under the table and sat down. I was pretending to fuss with JJ but what I was really doing was trying to put myself in Frank's place and figure out what he might be thinking. We go back a long way, Frank and myself; neighbours and school together since we were kids and a long spell in London in the seventies and eighties. There's not a lot we don't know about each other but I could tell that evening I had him fairly flummoxed.

"You were gone a few days," he said, not taking his eyes off JJ.

"A few days," I said. "Out foreign."

"Out foreign?"

"Out foreign."

He wasn't happy. He tried another tack.

"I thought there might be something wrong."

He was still staring at JJ. He told me afterwards it was as much as he could do to stop himself from reaching out with his hand to touch him and make sure he was real. Leaning out on his elbows he was, staring at him. I turned JJ round to face him.

Fifteen months later the liquidation of Interskan Shipping brought the vessel to the attention of the European Penal Commission. Its three-thousand-metre hold met the specifications of those architects on secondment to the EPC. Purchased at scrap value, renamed and registered, the *Somnos* spent the autumn of that year in Odense being refitted as a high-security neuro-intensive-care unit. On the twenty-fifth of May, after a three-week voyage, the *Somnos* was piloted into

16

"Say hello to your new neighbour, JJ. Frank, this is my son, this is JJ O'Malley."

I held out JJ and Frank drew back in his chair.

"Anthony . . . ?" He had his hand out, pointing. "Anthony . . . how, where . . . ?"

I could barely keep from laughing.

"I bought him," I said casually.

"Christ!"

"Two thousand dollars, give or take a few pounds, import duties and all the rest."

"For God's sake, Anthony!"

"What?" I said, playing the innocent. "You don't think it was a fair price. I thought it was a fair price."

You could see the colour rising in Frank's face. Go to the dresser, I said, and get the bottle. He poured two stiff ones and drew in his chair. It was my turn to start talking and now that it was I didn't know where to start. The more I thought about it the more I realised that some stories are so daft it makes no difference where you start telling them. You might as well start at the end as at the beginning because one part is as far from making sense as the next. But I had to start somewhere so I just took it out of face. I told him how, after the cattle had been taken away, I'd had a lot of thinking to do. Six months before I could stock up again, what was I to do in the meantime? Night after night in front

---

Killary fjord and dropped anchor in twelve fathoms of water. In line with naval protocol, captaincy of the ship was handed over to Norris Whelan, vice-governor of the Irish prison system. Three weeks of system checks followed, during which trial telemetry was relayed over the Astra satellite to Beaumont Hospital.

of the fire thinking and mulling things over, looking at the telly and trying to make sense of things. I told him how I'd seen the coverage of all those revolutions and those orphanages and how I'd got the idea of going abroad and getting a child of my own. Money wasn't a problem, I had my own house—what else would I do with it all? So I told him about the trip to that bitter city and all the days spent traipsing from one orphanage to the next with no clue what I was looking for. And then I told him how I found JJ and the wicked witch and about the haggling as well. No more than JJ years later, Frank could hardly believe it either, you could see it in his face. But I wasn't ashamed of it. I wasn't ashamed of it then nor am I now and that is something I cannot explain. He was quiet for a while after that and then he shook his head.

"I've heard some good ones in my time but I can say in all honesty I've never heard the beating of what you've just told me." He laughed. "And I never figured you for the fathering type, Anthony."

I shrugged. "There it is, you see, you never know. Spend enough nights on your own thinking and you start seeing things about yourself. You see the things you've done and the things you're likely to do and when you see that the balance of your life is already in the past you find you've got some hard decisions to make. You either face up to it or you settle down to pissing away what's left of yourself. There were nights here when that fire never went out."

It all sounded a lot wiser than I felt but it seemed to make sense at the time.

"He's a fine child though," Frank said. "How old did you say he was?"

"Two years old, he'll be two years old in the middle of April. At least that's what I've been led to believe."

"And he's healthy and everything?"

"He seems to be, there's nothing wrong with his appetite."

We talked on for another hour and it must have been near eight when Frank got up and put his glass on the table. Maureen would call over in the morning, he said. By that time JJ was flat out in my arms, his eyes closed and his mouth open. I put him in my bed next to the wall with two pillows outside him so he wouldn't roll over in his sleep and end up on the floor. He looked comfortable in that big bed, all warm and peaceful with the blankets pulled up under his chin. I put the light out but left the door open and when I got back into the kitchen I saw the two empty glasses on the table. I was happy that on his first night in his new home someone had already drunk to his health and happiness.

Maureen came over the following morning. We'd been up about an hour, JJ was fed and the fire was down when she opened the door. She passed straight by me to JJ, picked him up and held him out at arm's length to get a look at him. That's Maureen's way—cut straight to the heart of things, no beating around the bush. A lot different to Frank in that way; he has to know the ins and outs of everything before he can make a move. I suppose that's what makes them a good team. Anyway, whatever it was she saw in JJ she took to him straight away.

"JJ," she cooed. "Aren't you the gorgeous little thing? Such dark eyes." She turned him round so that the light fell on his face. "You're going to break a lot of hearts with those eyes, JJ, isn't that right, Anthony?"

Breaking hearts was something I knew nothing about so I kept quiet.

"How has he settled in, Anthony? Is he making strange with the place?"

As far as I knew he seemed to have settled in fine. I'd woken up that morning and found him sitting up in the bed beside me, looking around him. The poor fella hadn't a clue where he was. I pulled him on to my knee and talked to him and don't ask me what I said to him but whatever it was it seemed to put him at his ease. After he was dressed and fed he sat on the ground while I put on a fire. I'd just finished when Maureen came in. Of course she saw problems straight away.

"Does he have any clothes but these, Anthony? These could do with a wash."

"Not a stitch but those."

"Well, don't go buying anything just yet. I have a load of things young Owen has grown out of. I know someone who'll make good use of them, don't I, JJ?"

It wasn't the first time I was glad to have Maureen Lally for a neighbour and it wouldn't be the last either. It was only a small thing, a child's clothes, but it made me think for the first time that I might have bitten off more than I could chew. What did I know about a child's clothes, or anything else for that matter? For the first time I had a feeling I had done something foolish. This wave of fright

20

came over me. If Maureen had taken JJ away with her at that moment and told me I was never going to see him again I wouldn't have raised a hand against her, that's how spooked I was. She must have seen the look on my face. She handed JJ to me and laughed.

"Children are simple things," she said. "Keep them clean and warm. The only thing they need after that is love."

She came back an hour later and tipped a black rubbish bag of clothes on the table. After separating them out in little piles she went through them piece by piece, telling me what would go with what and holding up little sweaters under JJ's chin and saying didn't that go lovely with his eyes and doesn't that suit his colouring and of course it was all lost on me. As long as he's warm and clean I kept telling myself.

She stripped JJ then and put on a little sweater and blue pants and he looked a lot brighter in himself; I hadn't realised how dirty those clothes were.

"We'll bin these old things, won't we, JJ?" Mauren said, throwing them into the black bag. "And we'll get you a nice new coat and wellies so you can go outside and play with our Owen. Wouldn't you like that, JJ? Of course you would. Anthony, you'll have to bring him over this evening to meet Owen, to see how they get on."

"I'm thinking of bringing him to the doctor tomorrow and getting him checked out. Tests and everything, whatever they do with kids. These health certs, I don't know if they can be trusted."

"Wait till Friday. Tomorrow is dole day, the town'll be packed. Friday morning will be quiet, you won't have to answer half as many questions."

And that was another thing. How was I going to explain JJ? However hard it had been to explain him to Frank, it was going to be a lot harder to explain him to the whole of Louisburgh. Middle-aged bachelors don't up and go to foreign countries every day of the week and arrive back with two-year-old sons under their oxter . . .

"How would you handle it, Maureen? If JJ was your child what would you say?"

JJ was standing with Maureen bending over him. She had him gripped by the shoulders and he was stepping forward awkwardly, pawing the ground with his foot like it might give way under him. Maureen looked up at me.

"He's your child, Anthony, you're his father now. What explaining is there?"

"There'll be talk, Maureen, you know the way people are."

"People will always have plenty to talk about. If talk is the only thing you have to worry about you'll get no sympathy here. People will always find something to talk about, won't they, JJ? One look at those lovely eyes and they'll all be jealous. They'll all want to know where they can get little boys like this." She scooped JJ up into her arms. "If you want something to worry about you need look no further than that fire. The way this little fellow is going he'll be up to every mischief in a few weeks. You need to screen off that fireplace as soon as you can."

She left after that and we were alone together for the first time with a whole long day ahead of us. JJ had found his feet by this time. He was gripping the leg of the table and bouncing up and down, pointing out things around him. It was nearly midday and from what I could tell it was a mild grey day outside. I pulled a second sweater on him and a cap down over his ears and took him out into the yard to show him around. There was no cold in it but the sky was down on the ground and every place was running with water. We went round the sheds and barns and I told him what everything was for and what animals lived where, showed him where the calves were penned and bucket-fed in the winter and showed him where I kept the geese before selling them off before my trip abroad. I told him I'd never keep geese again because they were dirty things but that I might get in a few ducks because ducks were better company around a house. Then we sat up on the tractor—an old Ferguson 35 it was. He got a great kick out of that, twisting and swinging out of the steering wheel for a while. Then we stood under the bales of hay in the hayshed and looked out towards the sea, out towards Achill and Clare Island. I lifted him up on my shoulders and showed him that the sea was black and that that was a sure sign of rain. Sure enough as we stood there it came rolling in over the land, a dirty big shower, hammering off the roof of the hayshed and frightening JJ and setting him to cry for the very first time.

There was over a year between them. Owen was February and JJ was the middle of April. And from the beginning they were like brothers.

Maureen was in the kitchen talking to Owen in the sitting room when we went over that evening. Bring him through till we see how they get on, she said. Owen was on his feet gripping the side of the couch, running this plastic tractor up and down the length of it. I sat JJ in the middle of the floor and stood back to see what would happen. The two boys looked at each other, sizing each other up, Owen with this narrow frown on his face.

"This is JJ, Owen," Maureen said. "Say hello to him, your new friend. Go and say hello to him, Owen."

She took Owen by the hand and led him over to JJ. I was nervous then, afraid for JJ. It seemed to me somehow that the balance of his life hung in that moment. If he could only make a friend then nothing would be impossible for him.

I needn't have worried. The two of them spent a few more moments sizing each other up and then Owen held out his tractor to JJ and JJ took it and turned it over in his hands and then put it in his mouth. And that's how it was, their first moment together—one of them giving over his tractor and the other fella trying to take a bite out of it.

That was the first day of their friendship, a friendship that joined them at the hip as they say. And a lot of it was down to Maureen; she became the mother JJ never had. Everyone knows he spent as much time eating and sleeping in Owen's house as he did in his own. But I didn't mind that, I needed all the help I could get. Good neighbours are a blessing and I knew from that first day I could rely on her. Looking back now I don't know how I would have managed without her.

Frank came in and saw them playing together on the floor. "The two men," he said happily. "The men they couldn't hang."

JJ's health checked out fine. His medical records listed shots and inoculations but Dr Ryan said he'd give him booster shots just in case. He took a blood sample from him and said he'd have the results back in a few weeks—he wanted to do some tests on him to see if there was anything like MS or whatever waiting for him down the line.

"But he looks healthy I have to say. A healthy lucky baby. He could do with a bit of feeding up but other than that there doesn't seem to be anything wrong with him. As I say we'll know more in a few weeks. How is he feeding?"

"He eats whatever I eat, he seems to have no problem. Spuds and meat and vegetables, plain food."

"Good. Just mash it up for him or cut it into small pieces. I'm going to prescribe a small tonic. Once a day after his dinner. Other than that he seems to be fine. Bring him in to me if he starts running a temperature or anything. If anything comes up in the blood tests or if I need more information I'll give you a call. If you don't hear from me you'll know everything is all right."†

I didn't get any call from him.

He was baptised about a month after that—that would have been about the middle of May. I didn't know whether he was baptised or not or what religious background he came from so I decided to do it just to be on the safe side.

It was a Saturday afternoon, a lovely sunny day and

---

† Too narrowly conceived as a notional boundary beyond which it is impossible to speak or relay information, the Event Horizon is more

there was good crowd in the church. Of course word had got out by then so everyone had turned up to have a look at him—his first public appearance so to speak. And he looked the part too. Maureen had come in that morning and smartened him up, put on his clothes and brushed his hair—a thing I could never do—and he was the smartest-looking little lad you've ever seen. He was six weeks with me by then and he'd come on in leaps and bounds. He'd got stronger and hardier and his face had filled out and as Maureen said it was the type of face that was quick to smile. Anyway, he walked hand in hand with me up the aisle to the christening font and there wasn't a gig out of him throughout the whole thing. As good as gold he was. The same couldn't be said for Frank, his godfather . . .

Maureen told me he was all nerves that morning. You'd swear it was himself that was being baptised, she said. Nothing would do him but to have a few stiff ones before he sat into the car for the church and I suppose the heat of the place got to him when he was inside because when he stood across the christening font from me he had this high colour in his face and a smell of whiskey off him that would knock a horse. Swaying back on his heels he was

fully understood as a structure determined within and without the nature of the *Somnos* project itself, a structure which functions as an endo- and exoskeletal support which upholds and inscribes the project as a site within which identities as ongoing processes morph and shift through spatio-temporal planes. And while it is itself both speculative and conjectural and its arrhythmic moods are ever likely to falter and decay, it is an interweaving of shards and fragments linked by suggestive coherences we are compelled to reason with.

with a smile on his face like a man who was going to burst into song at any moment. Maureen gave him a shot of the elbow and that woke him up and he looked around him like he didn't know where he was. Then he started rooting in his inside pocket and pulled out his tobacco and a box of matches. For a split second I thought he was going to roll up a fag and throw the match into the christening font. Maureen looked like she was going to split him. Father Scallen was looking at Frank and Frank was looking off into the distance like he had other things on his mind. Then he turns the pack of tobacco over in his hand and takes out this folded handkerchief from under it and blows his nose. The whole lot back in his pocket then and that was it. It was as much as I could do to stop laughing. But everything passed off smoothly after that. Frank and Maureen forswore Satan with all his works and empty promises and JJ was held out so that the holy water could be poured over his head. He lashed out with his hand and nearly drowned us and everyone got a great laugh out of it.

When all the fuss was over the five of us went for a meal in the hotel—Owen was with us as well. A lovely evening it was too, sitting round and having a quiet drink and the craic and people coming up shaking my hand and wishing us well.

While the Event Horizon lies beyond an appeal to scholarship, evidentiary texts, archival research, the historical record, etc.—marginalia as a buttressing authority—as an attempt to describe a definitive circumference around any singularity it will always fall short as a final statement of containment. Any site wherein identities are stressed and deliquesced beyond their stand-alone sovereignty, any site which facilitates the neither-here-nor-there ontologies of imaging and information technologies, will always resist such delimitative attempts.

And when Maureen took the two boys home myself and Frank moved into the front bar and I bought a round of drinks for the house. It must have been near eleven when Frank gave us the first song. He could hardly stand by that time but no matter how drunk he is he's still a fine singer. "The Streets of Laredo," that's his song. He got the hush and he just stood there with his eyes closed and one elbow on the counter and it was no hardship to listen to him. The odd shout of Good man, Frank, and Shhh and Give him a chance and then at the end a big round of applause and someone said Folla that and I was called to sing. And that was it for the rest of the night. We sang it out, one after another along the bar, some of us singing twice and the night ended where it began with Frank singing "The Parting Glass." We were the last to leave—Johnny was wiping down the tables. When we stood out on the street the town was quiet, no one around except Sergeant Nevin standing on Morrison's Corner with a flashlight in his hand. Goodnight, men, he said as we passed and we went on our way down to the bridge where the car was parked.

It was around that time I applied for this council house. John Ryan was the welfare officer at the time; he was calling round fixing up JJ's medical card and children's allowance and so on. It was him that mentioned it.

There was only two bedrooms in the old house: JJ's behind the fireplace and mine at the other end of the house. It was big enough for both of us but you didn't need to do much looking at it to know it was no place to raise a child in. There was a small bathroom off the back and a flat-roofed kitchen extension put on in the seventies that was never right. It needed rewiring and the roof needed to be redone. I talked about renovating the whole thing.

"That's only throwing good money after bad," John said. "The sooner you get in an application for a council house the sooner you'll be out of this place. Take it from me this house will be down around your ears in a few years. It's no use reroofing or rewiring, a house this old will always be an old house, dampness and everything. Do the job right or forget about it. A child in your care and site on your own land—the whole thing'll be ready in a few months."

So I took his advice, wired off a half-acre of land—this half-acre we're on here—and filed for planning permission. Pete Mangan was peace commissioner at the time and he signed for it and the whole thing was in progress about two months later. It went out to tender that August and the foundation was dug and poured in the middle of September. John Finn put up the blocks and Ted Naughton—this was one of his first jobs—did all the plumbing and wiring. The promise was that we'd be in it by Christmas but between one thing and another it wasn't till the first week in February we turned the key in it.

JJ was nearly three years old by then. He'd grown strong and hardy and he was running around and up to all sorts of devilment; it was a full-time job keeping an eye on him. Up on tables and ladders and you couldn't keep him down off the old Ferguson for love or money. And one day, when my back was turned, he went missing. Owen came over looking for him and my heart came up in my mouth; I thought he was with him. Out we went looking for him, the whole lot of us; Maureen and myself going through the sheds and barns and Frank, grey in the face, standing on the wall of the slurry pit with a length of four-by-two in his hand. Then Maureen comes round the house with JJ asleep in her arms. Up on top of the bales she'd found him. How a three-year-old gasúr managed to climb up there with no ladder was beyond me but climb up he did. Up after the cat he'd gone and whether it was the heat of the hay or that he couldn't get down Maureen had found him asleep with the cat curled up on his belly.

That's when I put him into the crèche. I couldn't keep an eye on him twenty-four hours a day, not with the few cattle I had and doing jobs and everything. Maureen mentioned the crèche but I was in two minds about it. The way I saw it I hadn't taken him out of one institution to land him in another.[†] Maureen laughed at me.

"It's not like that, Anthony. It'll only be for a few hours a day, and besides, all those other kids there, it'll only be good for him."

I knew what she was saying but I still wasn't convinced. She must have read my mind because she told me then that she was thinking of sending Owen off for a few hours in

_____

† Footnoted beneath the Twin Towers collapse the *Somnos* takes its place amid the gathering iconography of twenty-first-century anxiety. Through reproductions on album covers and as a generative image in cultural studies it will achieve universal recognition. Filed in media memory it will become the nation's first image of the new millennium to achieve such instant recognition.

Centered in the surrounding darkness of the fjord, the ship's security and navigation lights give it the incandescent appearance of an alien spacecraft, strobing and numinous with first-contact immanence.

the morning and afternoon just to get him out from under her feet.

That settled it. JJ and Owen were packed off to the crèche till two in the afternoon when Maureen and I took turns picking them up and bringing them home. It worked out well enough. We'd get our day sorted out before they came home in the afternoon and put everything up in a heap and, as Maureen said, it was only for a few months, before they were packed off to school proper in September.

JJ and Owen were solid buddies by then. They went to school together in the morning and came home together in the evening and sometimes it was as much as I could do to keep JJ here of an evening and spend a few hours with him. But he needed so little. As long as he was fed and foddered and had Owen, his right-hand man beside him, he didn't want for another thing. Often, just so that I could spend some more time with him, I'd have Owen over for the dinner in the evening and the two of them would sit there at the table, laughing and talking and planning away together like two old men. Sometimes, looking back, I think it was Owen who reared JJ, not me. There was a brightness about him whenever he was

---

Its pallid occupants have come among us with their refined metabolisms and liminal communiqués from some higher-order teleology beyond our imagining. And while they are unlikely to play out the classic scenarios—stripping the planet of mineral resources, conscripting our womenfolk into some ghoulish reproductive project—they have already started to assimilate a whole culture. With all media commandeered and their names on everyone's lips there is already something worshipful in our gaze. We are ready to move on, beyond our childhood's end, into some transcendent forgetting of ourselves.

with him, a glow, as if the happiness in his soul was coming out in his skin. Now with all that's happened since I sometimes find it hard to find that happy JJ. All I seem to remember are the arguments and the heartbreak and the confusion we had later on. But for those few years he was happy and whatever part I had in it, if I never do another thing with my life, I will always be proud of that.

FRANK LALLY

I drive out once a week to the Killary to look out at that ship. Usually in the middle of the week when it's quiet because at weekends you can't get parking along that road with all those tourists taking pictures and looking out with binoculars . . .

I try and picture JJ out there on that ship, JJ and those other lads wired up to those machines and somewhere along the way I've found myself praying for him.[†] He'd get a laugh out of that, the same JJ. Everyone knows that he himself has no truck with that kind of thing and to tell the truth it was news to me that I did. It just happened one day when I was standing on the old pier looking out at him. Without thinking about it or anything I said a small prayer for him and it was over and done with before I realised it. It was news to me that I believed in God; I've never given that sort

---

[†] The images are by now familiar, part of the nation's dreaming. Shot in real time and relayed across five countries and four time zones they come across, even in memory, as pure theatre. Solemnised and ritualised, the live transmission shows them walking down the slipway in single file. Spaced at three-yard intervals and moving between the guards on the pier side and the soldiers in the slipway.

Point man is twenty-four-year-old Swede Haakan Luftig. One-time leader of Doctrinal Corpse and boy soldier in the Scandinavian death-metal wars of the early nineties, he now stands convicted

of thing a lot of thought. As long as a man has his health and everything around him is going middling then it's up to him to get on with it and make the best of things, that's what I've always thought. But I surprised myself that day standing there with that little prayer for him. Now, and for whatever reason, every time I go out there to look at him I always find myself saying a prayer. JJ needs all the goodwill he can get and if people like me don't do it, who will?

People will tell you that JJ was a lucky lad, a lucky child having the life he had compared to what it might have been; that's one of those careless things people say without thinking. But he wasn't and he isn't. JJ's never had a day's luck in his life. Anything that was given to him with one hand was taken away with the other. You've only to look back at all the time that lad spent in hospital when he was a child or to that day in the church to see that he would never have a day's luck in his life . . .

There were only a few of us in the church that day. It was the middle of a Sunday afternoon and JJ and Owen were

of four charges of copyright infringement. Six foot four, goateed and expressionless, his long-distance stare is fixed on a point somewhere in the middle of the fjord. His T-shirt, stencilled in fifty-two-point Day-Glo Gothic, tells us that Christ is a Cunt.

Behind him comes Emile Perec, twenty-four and convicted in Lille of seventeen driving offences while in charge of a public-school bus. In the grey light Perec has the pallid look of one who has spent too much time under artificial light—a snooker player or lab technician perhaps. Beneath his outsize shirt, however, is the greyhound physique of a man who at one time represented the future of French middle-distance running.

making their debuts as altar boys. It was a bit of an occasion, as you can imagine, otherwise I wouldn't have been there. Nor would Anthony either who was beside me in the seat. It was afternoon benediction and the idea was that the two boys would have their first try-out in front of a small audience; if anything went wrong there wouldn't be too many people to see it and not much embarrassment for the lads. All I remember hoping was that it would be over quickly and that we'd get away to watch the second half of the match—Mayo were playing Sligo that day in the Connaught final.

A few minutes before three JJ walked out of the sacristy carrying this long taper to light the candles on the altar. There was these two candelabra things at either end of the altar, ten candles on each of them reaching up to the centre in a kind of arch effect. JJ lit the right-hand one first, standing and leaning on his tiptoes to reach the last two or three. Then he went over to the one on the left. He lit the first five or six and was stretching up to the top ones when it happened. The cuff of his surplice must have caught on one of the lower candles. As quick as lightning this orange flame shot up his sleeve towards his shoulder. JJ jumped down from the altar shaking his arm, trying to put out the flame.

Third up is Jimmy Callanan, a twenty-six-year-old Scottish nationalist, sentenced to fifteen months at the Old Bailey for driving a white Mercedes bearing diplomatic number plates and tax and insurance discs registered to the Republic of Pictland—a two-acre field of scrubland outside the town of Arbroath.

Second last is Didac Jorda. Sporting the colours of FC Barcelona, he is the only one with a smile on his face. His career as a locksmith with *los servicios sociales de Cataluña* is on hold while he serves out an

Of course this only made things worse, fanning and spreading the flames to the rest of his body. I was out of the seat in a shot, racing up the aisle, pulling off my jacket. JJ was now dancing around in front of the altar, waving his arms and screeching, almost covered in flames—you'd think to look at him he'd just grown these big orange wings. I threw the jacket over him and wrestled him to the ground. It seemed like all this went on about half an hour but from the moment he walked out with the taper in his hand to the moment I put the jacket over him I'd say less than a minute and a half had passed. When I turned him over on his back he was all black and smoking. His surplice had been burned away entirely but as far as I could see there didn't seem to be too much wrong with him. He just lay there black and charred with smoke rising off him. Anthony pushed me aside and Father Scallen came charging out of the sacristy. Anthony had JJ sitting up with his arms around him.

"JJ!" he shouted. "JJ!" He put his hand under his chin and turned his face up. "JJ . . . !"

JJ just sat there wreathed in smoke and I saw that the hair on the side of his head and across his scalp had been badly singed.

---

eight-month sentence for carrying a concealed weapon inside the Bernabeau Stadium.

Last up is JJ O'Malley. Eyes fixed to the ground, he moves with a stiffness which has everything to do with an easy sense of embarrassment at being the focus of such drama. The clueless onlooker would pick him out as the one carrying the most grievous sin. It is all the more ironic therefore that he is the only one of the five not carrying a criminal conviction. His very innocence, in fact, is one of the conditions of him being here as he is.

"Stand back, let him have some air."

Maureen pushed into the crowd, shoving us aside. "Get him something to drink. Owen, get him a glass of water."

JJ was sitting there with no sound out of him. There were these long weals along the backs of his hands but they didn't seem to be giving him any pain. Maureen took his hands, turned them over and lifted his face so that she could see the marks on the side of his head.

"This child needs the hospital," she said. "These hands are going to blister. Get this black thing off him."

Anthony sat in the back of the car with JJ on his knees wrapped in a coat. Maureen sat in beside me and I put the boot down. We were lucky it was a Sunday afternoon—there wasn't any traffic on the road and we pulled into casualty about thirty minutes later. The nurses whisked JJ away with them and Maureen strode off behind them telling them she was his aunt.[†] I was alone in the corridor then with nothing to do except get a cup of tea and try to read the Sunday papers. There were only a few people in the coffee shop—a

---

[†] They drift in from the wings, rotating through six-hour shifts, the supporting cast of neuro-ICU nurses. Moving in the hyphenated time-lapse motion of the webcast there is something of the crisis apparition about them. Their white uniforms, fluorescing on our screens and monitors beyond accurate definition, lend them this aura of electedness.

A hand-picked elite, lured here by professional curiosity and a time-and-a-half pay deal, they shepherd their charges one on one through the cloudless echoing topography of this three-month interregnum. Their own essential cluelessness, the impossible empathy gap, proves no hindrance to the essential tasks of provisioning and orienting their subjects through the staging posts of this journey.

Confidentiality clauses bind them into their supporting role. However, like any elite happy in their work, they have their own anthem. Stitched

few patients going around in dressing gowns and a few gasúrs running about the floor with bags of crisps and ice lollies. Maureen and Anthony came back after about two hours. They looked a bit happier in themselves.

"He's settled now," Maureen said. "He'll sleep for the rest of the day."

"What did they say?"

"They said he was a lucky lad. Just his hands and his hair. They think he might have some scorching on his lungs but they'll do tests on that tomorrow."

"Did he say anything himself, did he talk?"

"He said a few words. Just that his hands were sore and that he had a hot feeling in his chest. But it doesn't seem to be troubling him too much. I think they are more worried about the shock than anything. They bandaged his hands and put something on his head. He's sleeping now."

Anthony pulled in beside me. "I'll come over in the

---

together from snatched phrases off the webcast, in five-part harmony and to the tune of "God Rest Ye Merry Gentlemen" . . .

> *MRIs wing through the skies*
> *On broadbands straight and true*
> *Drawn down to LEDs*
> *Plasma monitors too.*
> *PETs and encephalographs*
> *All our readings true*
> *Oh-oh tidings of comfort and joy*
> *Comfort and joy*
> *Oh-oh tidings of comfort and joy.*

It needs work but it's to their credit that they'd be the first to admit it.

morning to check on him. I suppose there's nothing else we can do for him this evening. The nurse said he would sleep till morning."

"There is nothing we can do," Maureen repeated. "I'll come over with you in the morning if you like."

I could tell Anthony was glad she'd said that. He drew his hands across his face and clasped them on the table in front of him. Then he spread them wide and looked at both of us. "Of all the things. And in a church too, of all the friggin' places."

I had no answer to that nor did anyone else either I'd imagine. I gathered up the paper and made to go. "It's just one of those things, Anthony. Nothing you or I or anyone else could have done."

Maureen and Anthony walked ahead of me to the car. A red-faced man with a little girl in a red dress was coming the opposite way. She was struggling under the weight of a big bunch of flowers. I asked the man how the game went. He threw his eyes up to heaven.

"A draw," he said. "They threw it away."

GERARD FALLON

The altar boy from hell?—yes, I remember that. Don't ask me who put it on him but from what I remember it was on him the first day he came to this school. The funny thing about it is that he never really was an altar boy. That day he went on fire and was nearly destroyed—that was his last day ever in a church as far as I know. But that's how it is in a small town like this, an incident like that can mark you in more ways than one.

I'd say in thirty years of teaching JJ O'Malley was the brightest young fella I've ever come across; the brightest by some distance. This school's never had a student with his abilities across the whole curriculum—our very own genius. Of course we'd seen those exam results of his and marvelled at them but it was one thing seeing them and another thing entirely coming face to face with the lad himself. There was nothing he wasn't good at, no subject he wasn't better at than any of his peers. Maths, physics, geography, literature, you name it, there was nothing he couldn't turn his mind to. He flew through any exam he ever sat without breaking sweat: brains to burn as they say.

But of course not everything interested him. The science subjects, maths, physics, chemistry—he had little enough interest in anything built on formulas or that argued towards definite conclusions. It was the discursive ones that drew him out and got him excited. English, history, religious instruction, civics—anything that led to argument and debate and multiple interpretation—that's where he was in his element. And of course he was the bookish sort too who liked flourishing big jawbreakers of words. Ontological for instance—you won't hear too many fifteen-year-olds coming out with that one. No, nor secondary school civics teachers either. I remember going to the dictionary for that one and I remember as well being none the wiser after I found it.

"There is an ontological and ethical priority established in the first paragraph," JJ repeated nervously.

"I'll take your word for it, JJ. But could you render that into plain English for the rest of us?"

He leaned forward on his elbows then, his hands clasped on the desk. This was a bad sign; JJ was about to get up on one of his hobby horses. If past form was anything to go by the class would pass in a blizzard of words and ideas and most of it would be lost on everyone around him. Still though, it was always worth seeing JJ vexed with the world and in full flow.

"The problem is that the constitution contradicts itself in the preamble, the opening paragraph. It recognises not itself but God as the Supreme Authority, the source of all laws including itself. The phrase . . ."

"I don't see the problem, JJ. The constitution is the bedrock of civil law in this country, just as it is in liberal democracies the world over."

"No, it is not and that is exactly the point. God is the foundation of civil law in this country."

He was clasping his hands under the table now to stop himself trembling. You could see he loved these discussions but you could see also that he was almost afraid of himself. He told me once he suffered from a kind of mind-racing— what he called his mindrot meditations. Sometimes ideas would come to him in the middle of the night and keep him awake till all hours, chasing after them to wherever they led him—up blind alleys and down dead ends as he put it himself. This sounded like one of them.

"Granted so that is the case, JJ. Go on. You're coming to the crux of your argument."

"Supposing someone was to stand up here in this classroom or somewhere else and claim that he was God and that he had evidence to prove that this was indeed the case. Then there would be a problem."

"Only if he disagreed with some article of the constitution."

"Exactly, suppose he did disagree. Suppose he woke up one morning vexed for some reason or hung-over from a feed of drink and he said give me another look at that constitution. So he reads through the whole thing and somewhere along the way, it doesn't matter where, he says stall the digger this has to be changed, I can't stand over this. So he takes out a pen and strikes through an article and rewrites it. Now in that case there wouldn't be a thing anyone could do about it, it's his constitution as it says itself. It wouldn't even have to go to the people."[†]

[†] Inhabiting the realm of the undead has not put the subjects beyond politics. How the project handed the public a silent media babe who

"JJ, if God were to appear here in the half-parish of Kilgeever He would have more things on his mind than amending the constitution. And as for sinking pints up in Thornton's . . . "

The class collapsed in guffaws.

"Spirits would be His drink, wouldn't it, sir?" someone called from the back of the class. "Top shelf."

"No," someone else said. "Wine would be His drink, wouldn't it, sir, that cheap Italian stuff? Or that stuff monks brew in monasteries. I'd say you couldn't keep it drawn to Him if He got started."

JJ looked down at his desk. I waited for the laughter to die down.

"JJ, if God were to sit down and rewrite the constitution there wouldn't be a problem. By definition God is all good and virtuous so anything He wrote would be on the side of good, both private and public, and hence unarguable. It would be interesting, however, to find out just how near or far our constitution diverged from the Divine Law. De Valera would be interested; he'd be up out of his grave in a shot."

"There wouldn't be a problem if God was true to your definition of Him . . . "

_____

has found broad approval across all demographics is one of its more interesting sidebars. Respondents to various newspaper and online polls have chosen JJ as the nation's favourite son, the man most likely to take any marginal seat in any forthcoming election—by-, general, presidential, or European. He now occupies a place in the nation's consciousness exceeding that of the project's original mandate. He is now public property and any attempt to appropriate him as the exclusive property of any single party is likely to be rejected by the electoral-

"You don't accept the definition? God is God, JJ."

"I'll go along with it for the sake of argument. The real problem arises if there is no God. Supposing someone was to stand up with definite proof that He did not exist—then the arse and foundation would fall out of the whole thing. All laws in this country would be groundless. No one would be bound by them any more."

"That doesn't follow. In that situation all we would be left with was the law of the land without divine source."

"No, this is an interim constitution. It is predicated on God's existence. It gets its authority from God and is directed towards God: it begins and ends in God. Now if God is absent then it collapses and has to be written again. We'd have to start from the beginning."

"Interim or not, JJ, it has served the country since 1937 . . . "

"With twenty-eight amendments."

"OK, twenty-eight amendments. That doesn't discredit it. Constitutional amendment is part of an evolving democracy. Even if I accept your argument the onus is still on you to prove that God does not exist and that is where you're stuck."

JJ shook his head. "My point is that there is a denial of

---

response reflex in cross-voting, abstention and outright hostility. The absence of any manifesto or electoral programme is seen as the perfect catch-all, a final and total collapsing of left and right paradigms, a deft clearing of the middle ground where the blunted spike and wave tracings of his EEGs assure us that, contrary to appearance, our man is bearing certain things in mind. Faced with a candidacy undreamt-of in focus groups or grass-roots soundings the government parties have found themselves hopelessly off-message. Baffling pollsters and

intellectual conscience in the constitution. The opening sentence, article six, it runs right through the whole document. The faithless are blackballed from the off and that is a denial of the very freedom and dignity it purports to uphold. It does not legislate for the faithless. Under its own terms they are quite literally unconstitutional or, to use Cearbhall O'Dalaigh's phrase, repugnant to the constitution. They can hardly be classed as citizens."

The bell went and the rest of the class began gathering up their books. Not for the first time they'd found themselves lost in the wake of JJ's reasoning. I needed a breath of fresh air myself.

"Time out, JJ," I said. "We'll continue this another day. Is this another of these mindrot meditations?"

"It was just an idea," he said, "just an idea I had."

"I'm impressed. You don't believe in God or the constitution?"

"It's not that I don't believe in them, it's just that I have no faith in them." His face brightened suddenly. "Suppose . . ."

I opened the door. "No, JJ. Suppose and suppose and suppose. Some other day."

*　　*　　*

running ahead of spin doctors, the political establishment now finds that mindlessness and the rhetoric of silence is likely to have a defining influence in the make-up of the next government.

By way of limbering him up certain nameless backers have already pitched him head to head in a five-way contest with the other subjects. A simple enough beauty contest it has, however, brought to light several unforeseen variables. Heavy online polling suggests that French national chauvinism is weighing in behind their man. Against that, how does one quantify the sectional loyalties of the worldwide death-metal

I often think of that discussion in light of what's happened these past three months. Everyone has a theory about JJ, not just here in this town but throughout the whole country. You know yourself all the think pieces and editorials that have been written about him. All that guff about the alienation of young men in a feminised world, trying to tie his coma into the rising number of suicides in eighteen- to twenty-four-year-olds. You could turn yourself inside out reading them and still have no clue at the end of the day who or what they were on about.

But if you ask me, JJ's problem was that he saw signs everywhere, he made too many connections, this was his difficulty. Everything that happened in his life—his time in the orphanage, his adoption, the burning in the church— he wove all these things together into a kind of world view. I suppose you could call it a philosophy . . . His abandonment by his mother and the circumstances of his adoption were only the start of it. He saw himself free in the universe, not in the positive sense of being able to make and forge his own destiny but in the negative one of being cast out without love or grace. Of course if you pointed out to him that he'd been rescued from something a lot worse he would have said that was just chance, he was lucky not

community? Will Jorda's pan-sexual appeal offset Spanish voter apathy? What of Callanan's canny pitch as a compromise candidate? Is JJ's homeboy status enough to see him breast the tape? All this above the protests of gay and feminist lobbies, disappointed ethnic minorities, all harping on themes of alienation and democratic deficit. The result is far from clear and as it stands it represents a considerable gamble on the part of JJ's backers. An ur-politics to be sure but still part of the nation's candlelit vigil.

worthy, and to JJ there was a world of difference. There was this want in him, this hunger—you could feel it in every discussion and debate we ever had. Argument for the sake of argument or point scoring didn't interest him; he had more need than that. He believed in everything he ever argued no matter how unlikely the idea. And that's why I don't think he was confused either. That's the kind of fool's pardon I find objectionable. I've never come across anyone with such a coherent sense of himself in the universe—it's something I can't explain, it just goes beyond me. But if that's confusion then it's the most reasoned and clear-sighted confusion I've ever come across.

SARAH NEVIN

You can see us together here in this photo. This was taken on the steps of the hospital the day I was discharged, three weeks after the accident. JJ with his arm around me and a big smile on his face, me with my bald head and crutches. It was the beginning of August, a beautiful summer's day, the sun splitting the stones. But see how pale I am, like a ghost; that was my first day in the sun that whole summer.

I like this photo, it's full of sunshine and it caught me at a moment when I was happy. More importantly, it caught me at a moment when I knew I was happy. I'm sixteen and a half in this photo, just back from the dead with a shiny new Kevlar plate in my head, a pair of crutches and two months' supply of opiate painkillers in my pocket. On that day, the eighth of August, I was the happiest girl in the world. My bones were mending, I had a recovery to look forward to and, best of all, I was in love.

What shocked me most was the amount of anger in him. I couldn't understand it. Everyone knows how Anthony took JJ out of that orphanage but not everyone knows that money changed hands. It made no difference to me when JJ told me. All I could see was that he was lucky to have been saved.

"Saved," he hissed. "For the umpteenth time, Sarah, I was bought, I wasn't saved. A herd of cattle went to the sword—well, the humane killer—for me. In the beginning was bovine spongiform encephalopathy."

"Don't be such a drama queen. How can you be so angry, it could have been a lot worse."

"How could it have been worse? You mean I could have changed hands for a consignment of fags or a colour TV. A fair exchange is no robbery."

"That's how it was, you said so yourself. It was chaos in that city. Riots, tanks in the streets, miners beating shit out of students. Revolutions are messy things."

"Revolution my tit. Revolution would be a fine thing. What kind of revolution starts by selling off its own kids? To this day no one knows whether it was a revolution or an internal coup. Imagine, you could go into any of those orphanages with a wad of used notes in your hip pocket and browse away to your heart's content till you found some child you fancied."

"Those orphanages were hell, JJ. Those kids have better lives now than anything they could ever have hoped for."

"How do you know? Have you ever wondered where some of those kids ended up? We were easy meat, Sarah, it was a free-for-all in those orphanages, like the new year sales. The US State Department estimates that ten thousand kids left that country in the immediate aftermath of the quote-unquote revolution. And they don't have a clue where they ended up. How many of them ended up in pornography or among paedophiles? No one knows, there were no checks or screening. As long as you had the spondulicks you were sorted. And of course if you came home and found that your little pink Caucasian baby was suffering from some illness you hadn't bargained for or that his chromosomes weren't stacked up the way God intended then you could turn him over to a state orphanage here, no questions asked. Twenty-three of us are now in orphanages here. AIDS, HIV, hepatitis, all the different shades of autism—bond with that! Some of us were so sick you couldn't quarantine us, never mind love us. It wasn't right, Sarah."

"You could be dead by now, JJ. Worse, you might still be in one of those orphanages, another state statistic. You should be glad you're alive and angry."

"Les irrécupérables," he said softly.

"What?"

"Les irrécupérables, that's what we were called. The irrecoverables. All of us lost to the world. Out of sight, out of mind."

"It wasn't your fault. You're not guilty of anything."

He turned away and I was left looking at his back.

"My point exactly, Sarah. I'm not guilty of anything, I'm just guilty."

This was the worst of him, all that anger and bitterness, it just kept chewing away at him. This going hand in hand with his mindrot meditations could make him hard work sometimes. The mindrot meditations; that's what he called those flights of fancy he would go off on sometimes. They could take hold of him any time, a chance phrase, a snatch of a song, a picture—it didn't matter, off he'd go spinning out a ream of rubbish for whatever length of time it took

50

for it to fade out under its own weakness. But, because they never resolved themselves in any lesson or insight, they frustrated him. That's why he called them his mindrot meditations. He had this idea that his own mind was eating itself up. He got the idea from reading an article on body-building. Seemingly, in the bodybuilding community it's common practice to starve yourself in the days before competition. The idea is that with no foodstuffs to process the digestive enzymes turn on the body itself and start consuming the fatty tissue and after a couple of days you get optimum definition. But sometimes the process goes too far and the body starts feeding on its own muscle and starts to rot from the inside out. JJ thought he saw this happening to his own mind. His mind or his soul was chewing itself up, eating itself back to its own substructure. Those flights of fancy, the remedial metaphysics as he called them, were only the first stage of its self-consumption. What would happen when his mind had burned off all that fat, what would happen when his mind had nothing to feed off but itself? What would happen then?[†]

One day we were at the sea, walking behind the pier. It

_____

[†] "Coma is a sleep-like state from which an individual has not yet been aroused."

Refined from the Hippocratic idea of coma as "a sleep-like state from which an individual *cannot* be aroused," LeWinn's definition facilitates the growing corpus of documented and anecdotal evidence which testifies to individuals making various degrees of recovery from deep coma. Furthermore, it accommodates the use of medically induced coma in certain surgical procedures.

Routinely used in cases of seizure and intracranial hypertension, barbiturate comas induce deep central nervous system depression

51

was quiet, just the two of us with the whole beach to ourselves. We were talking about the Killeen further up the shore. The Killeen in this parish, where all the stillborn and unbaptised babies were buried, was dug in a field behind a cliff face which looked out to sea. But over the years coastal erosion had eaten back the cliff face and disturbed some of the graves. Sometimes after storms and high seas people found little skulls and bones strewn along the sand. I said something about how terrible this was, how painful it must be for people with loved ones buried there. Of course JJ saw it differently.

"Maybe those kids want to go back to the sea. That's where we come from in the first place, isn't it? Maybe they want to start all over again. Washed out to sea and broken down by the sand and water, then rising up into the clouds and falling as rain all over this green and pleasant land. Rising up again as grass and trees and nettles and briars, maybe that's what they want."

"That's a JJ idea. I don't see it myself. If you're dead you're dead and that's all there is to it. No longing or feelings."

----

beneath level-three thresholds of surgical anaesthesia. A medium IV dosage of 10mg/kg/hour of Thipentol maintains the subjects in the deep end of the Glasgow Coma Scale. The delta wave signature of depressed synaptic activity at this level lies within a spectrum of 0.3—5HZ. The duration of the coma is reckoned within such recovery indices as the resumption of normal intracranial pressure and against such limiting factors as acute muscular atrophy, cardiovascular and renal damage. In the case of the *Somnos* project a further limiting consideration is that one-third of all inmates in Irish prisons serve an average of three months.

"They don't belong there, Sarah, it's not sacred ground, it's not even consecrated. And I'll bet they know it. I'll bet they're happy when they're washed up out of those graves. Imagine how they must feel when they get out of that cliff, when they feel the starlight and fresh air on their little skulls. I'd say they get a whole new lease of life. I'll bet if you came down here some moonlight night you'd see them, all these little skeletons, jumping around and dancing and singing their little heads off. And then, just before sunrise, they run down to the waves and swim out to sea until their arms tire and they sink gladly down to the seabed. I'll bet if you came down here some moonlit night that's what you'd see."

I shuddered. "I wouldn't want to see it. It wouldn't make me one bit happy. Besides, those little kids won't have much more time for singing and dancing. The whole thing is going to be exhumed and relocated to the new graveyard."

"That's a mistake, I'll bet that no one has considered what those little kids want."

I threw up my arms in exasperation. "That's rubbish, JJ."

"Is it? Suppose one night one of those little skeletons paid you a visit. Suppose you woke up and found one of them

---

Speculation has been voiced that the growing use of barbiturate comas in cases of radical surgery is now dictated by insurance rather than clinical concerns. The worrying incidence of litigation from patients who, following resuscitation after surgery, testify to consciousness of acute agony while undergoing surgery is now seen as a defining consideration as to the level and type of anaesthesia used in surgical theatres. The medical community deny that medical procedures are compromised by cost-benefit considerations.

sitting on the end of your bed. He has a job for you he says, he wants you to speak on their behalf. He's heard about relocating the Killeen but himself and his buddies want no part of it. They're happy where they are, or happy in so far as dead kids can be. They're prepared to take their chances with the sea, they see it as a second chance and they are willing to take it. He wants you to be a spokesman for the dead, to make a moving plea on their behalf. After listening to him for a while you agree to make representation on their behalf, you make no promises but you tell him you'll give it a try. Of course the little fella is delighted. He shakes your hand and turns to go but you have other ideas. You don't want him to leave. It's not often you're on speaking terms with the dead; you have a lot of questions. You don't want to pass up this chance.

"'So what's limbo like?' you blurt out before you can stop yourself.

"The little fellow turns round and shakes his head. He hadn't expected any questions but now that his work is done he's in no hurry.

"'A terrible place,' he says. 'Badly thought out, a real rush job. There's no facilities or toys or anything. It's like an open-cast copper mine. We just sit around talking all day and night but since all of us are kids we have nothing to talk about.'

"'So who looks after you, who feeds you, do you ever see the angels?'

"The little skeleton fellow is standing inside the door. He has loads of time.

"'You'd see angels once in a while; you'd see them passing

through. Some of them are OK, the lesser ones, the thrones and dominions and virtues, they're OK, they don't have too many airs about them. They might stand and pass a few words with you but mostly they just pass through. But then there are the others, Gabriel for instance, deafening everyone with his bugle. And then there's Cupid—'

"'You've met Cupid!'

"'Yes, but you wouldn't know him now, he's put on a lot of weight.'

"'Has he? I could well imagine. I mean, any picture I've ever seen of him, the thick arms and legs of him, you could tell he was going to have a problem with it later on.'

"'He has a problem now all right. And he's angry and bitter with it. You couldn't listen to him. Moaning and griping and bitching about the glory days when he was a marksman and could hit a target at a thousand paces. He couldn't hit the ground now if he fell. And of course it's everyone's fault but his own.'

"'Jesus!'

"A funny look crosses his bony face.

"'No.' The little fella shakes his head. 'I've never met him, or met anyone who has either. You hear a lot of talk, stories and so on, but I have yet to meet anyone who has met him.'

"'And what about the other fella, the red gent with the horns and the pitchfork—'"

"JJ!"

"What?"

"Shut up."

"I was just coming to the good bit."
"No! I don't want to hear any more."
And that's what a mindrot meditation was.

KEVIN BARRET TD[†]

There was never a percentage in it, not in terms of public profile or column inches or first preferences or anything else either. That was obvious to me the minute my senior colleague landed that project on my desk—a blue folder with the word SOMNOS stencilled on it. I didn't know what the word meant then but I do now and when I read through it I thought of what that journalist said to me that day on the steps of the Dáil: a poisoned chalice right enough.

No, I didn't wonder at it or think twice about it and I'll tell you why. On the evening I got my portfolio I was sitting in the Dáil bar talking to Emmett Cosgrave—he was junior environment minister at the time and he told me a story which has stood to me since. Emmett was back from an

---

[†] . . . the total valid poll divided by the number of seats plus one, plus one . . .

Fifteen years teaching fractions and percentages in a two-room national school have given Kevin Barret a keen appreciation of the division of notional entities. The breakdown of votes in this marginal constituency is of a piece with such abstract divisions. Against history and demographics, reasoned analysis and projections, he has successfully waged three general elections on a core vote which has risen and dipped like a cardiograph within a bandwidth of plus and minus two points. And each victory has come narrower than the last; all of them late-night dogfights into the early hours, eighth and ninth counts, Kevin transferring from independent and single-issue candidates till

environmental conference in Düsseldorf, of all places. He'd put in a hard morning's work in front of some watchdog committee explaining why this country wasn't meeting EU legislation in agricultural pollution and groundwater contamination. Emmett had pointed to pending legislation and greater enforcement of existing laws and so on. All morning on the defensive and that wasn't the half of it. In the afternoon, as part of a subcommittee, he'd met a delegation of Green Party activists from France and Germany concerned about the levels of mercury emissions from crematoriums throughout the EU. Seemingly, crematoriums are the single biggest violators of mercury emission codes across the whole EU, bigger even than heavy industry which, by and large, has cleaned up its act. But because of what they do crematoriums have managed to escape censure and this is what was worrying these people. Now I didn't know there was mercury in the human body. There isn't, Emmett said, or at least there shouldn't be. But there is mercury in prosthetics: breast implants, pacemakers, false limbs, false teeth,

---

that hushed moment when the returning officer mounts the rostrum and announces him elected to the fifth and final seat in this, the most far-flung and sprawling of all Irish constituencies.

And he has now risen without trace. Dáil records show that while his attendance is exemplary the same records have no memory of him ever having tabled a question, participated in a debate or served on any of the committees or subcommittees which make up the day-to-day business of government; his presence is little more than spectral. However, with an eye to the upcoming general election the party's director of elections drew up a list of likely seat losses and, for the first and only time in his political career, Kevin Barret's name headed a list of likely candidates. Securing this marginal seat at the price of a junior ministry was thought to be a fair exchange.

teeth fillings, glass eyes, glasses, hearing aids and God knows what else we've been fitting ourselves out with. And with an ageing and more beauty-conscious population across the EU there are no shortage of these. The problem arises when crematoriums cannot burn off the latent mercury in these things. If a crematorium burns above a certain temperature, there's no problem—the mercury vaporises and condenses within the incineration process, it can be gathered and disposed of safely in toxic dumps or, you'll be pleased to know, because of its refinement, there is a ready market for it in the pharmaceutical industry. But if crematoriums do not reach this temperature, the mercury flies off in a raw state into the atmosphere and does all sorts of damage to the ozone layer and so on. Now since 80 percent of crematoriums across the EU were built in the sixties and seventies they are operating systems which cannot reach these temperatures and therein lies the problem. And make no mistake about it, there is a problem. Listening to these people, Emmett said, you'd think the planet was choking on the fumes of burning breast implants and glass eyes.

It was not a popular decision. The night of the cabinet reshuffle, deputies with longer and more distinguished party service drank sullen pints and said they couldn't understand it. A rank outsider like Barret, a man with no form or pedigree coming from the back of a quality field, now finding himself being rubbed down in the winners' enclosure . . . They were right but not in the way they thought. They could not understand Kevin's game and even if they had they would, more likely than not, have baulked at the degree of nerve and patience needed to play it to this end. Had they been in his kitchen the night he'd received the party nomination and watched him dividing up an Ordnance Survey map of the constituency with a ruler and pen they might have had some inkling.

Three and a half hours he sat listening to this. Facts and figures and demographic charts, medical submissions and forward projections . . . By his own account Emmett lost interest after the second hour and began worrying about catching his flight home. But, when it came to winding up the discussion, he thought he saw an opportunity to win back some of the ground he'd lost earlier in the day. He conceded that while he saw there was a problem and indeed a serious one, it was not an Irish problem. Ireland does not have a cremation culture; to the best of his knowledge there is only one crematorium and this one operates within existing codes. Obviously therefore the problem did not concern us. This was where they had Emmett snookered. As an addendum to their presentation they produced a proposal which outlined the need for biodegradable cardboard coffins and unbleached cotton shrouds for those countries with a burial culture. Would Emmett be tabling a motion in the future to bring these proposals to effect? This was too much for Emmett. He gathered up his papers and left the room.

"It's not power, Sadie," he said to his wife. "That's not what this is about. Power is compromise and horse trading and that's all bullshit. What I want is influence, the word in the ear, the private audience. Nothing on paper, no comebacks or queries but the job getting done just the same. Nothing to show you ever had a hand or part in anything but a letter in the post telling them that the road will be fixed, the medical card is in the post and thanking them for their support in the future. That's what I want, Sadie, getting things done without getting bogged down."

And that's how Kevin Barret found himself standing as one of four new junior appointees on the steps of the Dáil, fielding questions from the poll corrs of the national press.

The following week when I read through the outline of the *Somnos* project I thought of that story. I didn't blink or wonder at it because I knew then it doesn't matter whether it's biodegradable cardboard coffins or prison ships in Killary harbour. It's all politics, a job of work to be done and the sooner you get over your astonishment the sooner you can do something about it.

I knew straight away that the sticking point of the whole project was never going to be the expense or the environment or other factors—it was the idea itself that would prove difficult to sell. A penal experiment in a county with the lowest crime figures in the country and the country itself with the lowest crime figures in the entire EU—this was the paradox which had to be sold to the electorate, the Irish people. It had to be put to them as starkly as possible; they had to be made see the necessity for it.

The fact that the Irish taxpayer was underwriting the whole thing gave me a degree of leverage. I thought I saw a loophole. Reading through it I couldn't see why the

---

"Mr Barret," a voice called. "What is your reaction to this surprise appointment? Coming to a department which is widely seen to be in chaos? Today's editorials say this appointment may be something of a poisoned chalice."

At this moment Kevin was thinking of his one-time football career. At his peak, a nip-and-tuck corner forward, he had once scored a goal and two points in a Connaught final. Two years later his career was cut short by a torn cruciate ligament in his left knee which to this day leaves him with a slight limp. His ambition to play in an All Ireland final would never be realised. Now he mused absently.

"When I was a footballer I always liked to get a few wallops early on in a game. That always woke me up. Then I knew I'd always go on to get three or four scores."

volunteers had to be exclusively prisoners—there was nothing in the original proposal stipulating that this had to be exclusively the case. Enquiring into it I found there was nothing in the constitution to prohibit someone who was not a prisoner from volunteering. That made me think. When I mentioned it at committee stage there was, what can only be termed, a sharp intake of breath among the other members. Don't even think of it was the unspoken plea. But I did keep thinking. The other participating countries were already well ahead of us in terms of finalising their nominees. All the logistics were in place, everything was ready to go. Already in some quarters we were seen to be dragging our heels despite the fact that we were underwriting the whole thing. All the time though I was thinking about that loophole in the protocol.

SARAH NEVIN

It was through JJ that I met Owen and got to be a part of what they were together. And of course like everyone else I knew that JJ and Owen were like brothers. It was common knowledge that JJ had been reared in Owen's house and that they had sat together in the same desk right from their first day at school together. But one look at them and you knew straight off they weren't real brothers—JJ with his sallow skin and dark eyes and Owen with his fair hair and summer freckles. But even so there was an uncanny close- ness about their friendship and I was wary about stepping into it as I did. It worried me that I might drive some sort of wedge between them and then both of them would end up resenting me and I would end up the loser on both sides. But it didn't come to that. Owen just moved aside and let me move into the vacant space beside JJ as if he'd been keeping it warm for me all the time. There was no jeal- ousy there, no awkwardness—that's how open-hearted Owen was.

Ten minutes in their company and you'd know why they got on so well together. People have it that JJ was the one with all the brains, the sharp one who read all the books and anguished over things. Owen on the other hand was the direct one, the one who refused to tie himself up in

63

knots over anything. That's the way everyone saw it: JJ the tortured brainy soul and Owen the man who lived in the moment with no care for broad metaphysical speculation as JJ put it. But that's only half the story. It tells you nothing of Owen's sharpness and common sense and it tells you less of how JJ envied him this laid-back attitude. JJ'd read some sprainbrain book or see something on telly and he'd be full of it for days afterwards, arguing it and discussing it and gnawing at it like a dog with a bone. Owen might see the same thing but he'd refuse to get bogged down in it, he'd make some comment and pass on. In those moments I always thought he was the smart one, the one with a sense of his own limitations. He'd be the first one to tell you he didn't have JJ's brains or learning but if you ask me he was the wiser of the two. The awful thing is that this difference, the very cornerstone of their friendship, was the very thing that came between them in the end.

When it was all over JJ told me he was convinced Owen had blundered into someone else's death. The way he saw it Owen should have lived a long happy life, married with a wife and kids, carrying on into old age and complaining of damp weather and arthritis. One night he'd lie down beside his wife and die in his sleep, passing over to the other side as calmly as he had done everything else in his life. If you'd known Owen you'd have known what he meant.

It was the summer after I got out of hospital and if there was something on that night I cannot remember what it was. Myself and JJ had spent that whole year together and we were happy. Sometimes we'd meet up in the evenings in one of the pubs in town; on this particular evening we were sitting in Thornton's when Owen came in. One look at him and I knew he was in bad form. Work—he was driving a tractor for Peter Monk that summer—was hard and the hours were long; he was still in his working clothes. He was limping as well, a football injury from earlier in the week, and it was still sore. But his main trouble was woman trouble. Earlier that summer he'd fallen for one of the American students who come to Louisburgh each year to do some module in Irish studies. Her name was Mary Gee, a blonde toothy girl from Minnesota who, as JJ said, smiled like she was advertising some new feminine hygiene product. Owen had fallen for her and was broken-hearted when she'd returned to America at the end of May. She'd left Owen some vague promise of returning in August and his hope was that she'd stay in his house for a month or two. He wrote to her every second day but her responses had been fitful at best. All he knew was she was now working in a bookshop in Duluth, hardly making the sort of money that would finance a return trip to Louisburgh. He'd sent her some money but there was no mention of that in any of her letters and he was beginning to get the feeling he didn't figure so much in her plans any more. And of course he was taking it hard. Most of JJ's friends would've had flings with these American students and most were glad to see the back of them when they returned to the States in late May. But Owen wasn't like that. He was seriously lovestruck and visibly pining. If you got him on his own with a few drinks on him it was nothing but Mary G this and Mary G that and Mary G the next thing. When he joined us that evening he was very down in himself.

We had a few drinks together and tried to cheer him up, but by closing time, he was no happier than when he came in. We were standing outside the chipper and JJ was making ready to walk me home. One look at Owen and my heart went out to him, I didn't want him going off on his own. I suggested we go back to the chalet; it was only just after twelve, there was bound to be some drink lying around. The two boys were up for it—with a few pints on them they had a lip for more drink.

The chalet is just back the road near to the pier. Dad rents it out in the summer so it's always a good bet for having a few bottles lying around. I remember as we walked in the gate the outside light came on. JJ swore.

"I hate it when it does that," he said. "No one asked it to do that."†

Sure enough there was loads of drink in the kitchen: a half-bottle of vodka in the cupboard, a bottle of wine on the worktop and a couple of cans in the fridge. But Owen wasn't interested in the cans or the wine. He'd found a bottle

---

† One of those places where we've got ahead of ourselves, taken leave of our senses. Our essential selves now move a couple of paces ahead of us, opening doors and switching on lights, tripping intruder alarms, motion sensors and biometric systems . . . our souls clearing a path through the technosphere for the trailing golem of ourselves. This is how we've become attenuated, how the borders of our identities are drawn out, vitiating our core selves; this is how we've found ourselves beside ourselves. One day we might come completely unhinged. Somewhere

of Wild Turkey at the back of the cupboard and he took it with a pint glass into the sitting room. JJ reminded him he had an early start in the morning.

"Fuck the start," Owen said. "Let's see how wild this turkey really is." He tipped a third of the bottle into the pint glass and I knew then he was going to drink himself into oblivion.

"Jesus, this knee." Owen winced and shoved JJ to the end of the couch with his boot. "Push over till I stretch out this leg." He bent forward to massage his knee. "Peter better get the clutch adjusted on his tractor or I won't be able to walk the rest of the summer."

We talked and drank for about an hour, Owen firing back the whiskey and getting steadily drunker, myself and JJ sharing an armchair across from him.

We fell quiet then, fatigue and the lateness of the night getting the better of us. Owen was leaning off the end of the couch, shading his eyes with his hand and nursing the glass on his knee. JJ was smoking away beside me, lost in his own thoughts. It was just the sort of mood for thinking out loud and of course JJ couldn't let it pass.

"Suppose you found out your life was an experiment," he said, to no one in particular. "Someone else's experiment."

---

beyond arm's reach our soul will turn round and wave goodbye to us before moving off and pulling the door behind it, leaving us here, under the fluorescent lights, with nothing to lean on save these vigilant machines with their unerring testimonies. It will have turned its back on us, with all our works and empty promises. Cored out in this fashion, ontologies and IDs reassigned, someone or something else will come to stand in our place . . .

Owen groaned. "Not this shite this hour of the night."

"I'm only saying," JJ said.

"No you're not. This is the old story, the world versus JJ O'Malley."

"Yeah, yeah."

I could feel JJ rising to the hint of an argument. I tried to head it off. "Don't butt heads with him, Owen. You know how he is."

"Yeah, Owen, I'm the one with the horns, remember."

Owen turned over on his side and settled his leg under him. "OK," he said, "it just so happens that I'm in the mood for a row. Bring on the prosecution. Who's at the head of the queue tonight, JJ?"

Fatigue and annoyance had emboldened Owen. I had never seen him squaring up to JJ before.

"Go on," he said. "This court is now in session, the Honourable Sarah Nevin presiding."

JJ leaned forward in the chair. There was no stopping him now. "He comes up to you in the street, someone you've never met before. He offers to buy you a drink . . ."

I raised a hand. "I thought this fella stood for the prosecution."

"It goes towards motive, Your Honour."

"We haven't all night, counsel, get to the point."

"Yes, Your Honour." He turned back to face Owen. "He takes you into Thornton's, into the front bar and buys you a pint. Just when you're supping your pint and wondering what this is all about he pulls out a sheaf of notes and shows you your life. It's all down there in black and white, your whole life in one long narrative. It contains every dream and thought you've ever had, every hope and injury you've ever had, everything right down to the fillings in your teeth. It's all there including the pint in front of you on the table, and the man across from you with the sheaf of notes who bought you the pint."[†]

"I'm getting dizzy. Where the hell is this going?"

Owen's patience was running out already, an angry heat flush rose over his cheekbones.

"He has bad news for you."

"What sort of news?"

"He's come to tell you that you've failed."

"Failed what?"

"You've failed generally. He doesn't have to go into the details."

"Talk about broad strokes. Failed what, the whole human race I suppose?"

JJ shrugged. "Yes, if you want, the human race, the mental handicap over a life and two furlongs. You've been a big disappointment. Certain people had expectations; you've failed to meet them and now they're washing their hands of you."

Owen swung his feet off the couch and tipped more whiskey into the glass. He waved the bottle in a wide arc.

[†] And of course stalking the margins of this whole thing the ultimate Event Horizon himself, that gaunt gent wardrobed out of a child's nightmare, tooled up with scythe and hourglass, this one-time hero of the medieval woodcut now rehabbed as the pin-up of choice in the worldwide death-metal community. He has fallen into step with the rest of the foot traffic through the broadband, those scholars still up burning the midnight oil: porn queens ranked by the star system; terrorists and arms dealers fencing the latest ordnance and intel; conspiracy theorists

"Back up a second. How do I know this fella is talking to the right fella? How does he know he's talking to the right fella? I can't just take him at his word."

"I've told you, he has your life story, everything about you down in black and white."

Owen shook his head. "He has nothing, it's purely circumstantial, on its own it will never get a conviction."

"Not on its own, but he has the forensics to support it. You've been sloppy, you've left traces all over the place—fingerprints, dental impressions, retinal scans, genetic signatures . . . It all corroborates the written evidence."

Owen guffawed. "He could be showing me anything. My dental impressions—oh yes I'd recognise them anywhere . . . I don't think so."

"What you recognise is neither here nor there. They can all be objectively verified. The margin of error in any single one of them is almost small enough to establish his case beyond reasonable doubt. All of them together pointing in the same direction . . . I'm afraid you're fucked."

"Bollocks! And he's only a bollocks as well."

I held up my hand. "The jury will disregard that last remark. Once more, counsel, and you will be in contempt."

"What about motive? So far the prosecution has failed

_____

handing out cautionary tales like market-square pamphleteers; mules weighed down with credit-card and RSI numbers; paedophiles with gender and sexual orientation turned the full one eighty; bedroom-floor traders drawn from their sleep on some limbic twitch—these are his fellow pilgrims at this late hour. And long in the tooth now as you might well imagine plus jaded from wading through the impedance of the night he is here nonetheless and is anxious to get on with the job at hand. It's easy to see what has drawn him here; this is

70

to establish any reason for this whole charade. No motive whatsoever."

"You've forgotten . . . you've disappointed him."

"I'll get over it, believe me."

"He's not so forgiving. In fact, that is why he's here. He's here to punish you."

"He's going to punish me? How's he going to punish me? Is he going to shoot me, a hit man? He's going to pull out a handgun in Thornton's bar and blow me away?"

"No, it's worse than that, just telling you is punishment enough."

"That makes no sense. You're saying that his evidence is the punishment. What sort of sentence is that?"

"It's the worst sort; you have to live with it."

Owen sat back on the couch. He was looking at JJ intently, shaking his head sorrowfully as if seeing something deeply pitiful for the first time. "You're always like this," he said softly, "always coming out with this sort of shite."

"Don't heed him, Owen, you know how he is."

Owen was near tears now, drink and tiredness suddenly overpowering him. His inspiration had dried up too and he knew it. He was looking at me, hoping I'd side with him.

"I know what I'd tell that cunt, I'd tell him what I'm

---

where consciousness is drawn down to its own pilot light, a votive flickering in its cranial grotto. Despite his years he still has it in his wrists; however, it's the tips of his fingers that ache to reach out now and pinch it over the threshold of clinical ontology, into the *dépasse* realm of civil rights infringement, medical liability, national outrage, past tense . . .

telling you right now. Fuck off back to where he came from, just like I'm telling you the same thing JJ. Fuck off, you and your big ideas."

"Badgering the prosecution, Your Honour."

"I'll badger the cunt right enough."

I could feel JJ stiffening beside me. He'd gone too far this time. He should have seen the signs. Owen was standing over us glowering, his face swollen with frustration and temper. He took a step towards JJ and then took two steps back. He swung up the bottle.

JJ said, "Take it easy, Owen. I was only thinking out loud." He held up his hands. "The prosecution rests."

Owen lowered his face into JJ's. "Fuck off, JJ, I'm not listening to any more of this shite. I'm going to bed." Owen moved towards the bedroom and JJ got up to follow him. I pushed him back.

"No, JJ, I'll go."

Owen was sitting on the side of the bed sobbing, the glass held between his legs. "Why is he always like that, Sarah?" he asked. "Why does everything have to be about him?"

"That's the way he is, Owen, you know him, he can't let anything go. Can you walk home?"

He shook his head and lay back on the bed. "I'm too drunk, my knee is too sore."

"Then stay here tonight, I'll set an alarm for you. Eight o'clock, that will give you six hours." I reached for the bottle but he clasped it closer to his chest. "Give me the bottle, Owen." He lurched up in the bed and drained off the last of the whiskey then fell back on the pillows.

72

"Go away, Sarah," he slurred. "Go away."

When I got into the kitchen JJ was leaning on the sink looking tired and sorry.

"Is he OK?"

"He's fine, he's asleep."

He threw his hand up in a sorrowful gesture. "I didn't mean anything."

"You don't know how hard it is to listen to you sometimes. You can be so righteous."

"I can't stop it, Sarah, it's the way I am. I didn't mean anything."

"You did, JJ. But not in the way you think."

I tidied up the tins and glasses and JJ looked in on Owen. He was lying on his side, breathing deeply.

"I've set the alarm, he'll be OK. Come on, it's time to go."

We walked home hand in hand that night. A big summer moon hung over Carramore Hill and the fields were bathed in this deep blue light; it was like walking through a cobalt bottle. JJ kissed me at the gate and told me he'd call me the following morning. Watching him walk away that night I don't think I ever saw him looking so sad.

JJ got a call from Owen's mother the following morning— Owen hadn't turned up for work. Peter Monk had been on the phone to her, where the hell was he? JJ told her he'd get him. He hopped into the car and called for me. I picked up the keys of the chalet and sat in beside him; JJ was effing and blinding.

"You're sure you set the alarm?"

"I'm sure. Maybe it didn't go off."

"Maybe. Maybe he's hung-over, the hoor, him and his Wild Turkey."

"His knee was bad. It's not like him to sleep in. Owen is as good as his word, hung-over or not."

"He better have an excuse. Peter Monk is in Lachta, up to his oxters in seven acres of grass."

There was no sign of life in the chalet. The curtains were still drawn and there was no cup drying on the sink. JJ threw open the bedroom door and shouted in.

"Owen, you lazy bastard, rise and shine."

I could see over JJ's shoulder. Owen was lying on his side, facing the window, just as I'd left him. I went over to draw the curtains. JJ drew a kick on the bed.

"Come on, you lazy hoor, get up."

When I turned around JJ was down on one knee over Owen. His face was blank and his left hand was poised a foot over Owen's shoulder. Owen's face was blue and open-mouthed, a small pool of black drool staining the sheet under his cheek.

"Owen!" JJ turned him on to his back and shook his shoulders with both hands. "Owen!" He struck him hard across the cheek and Owen's head spun slowly through ninety degrees. "Owen! Wake up to fuck!"

I pushed JJ aside and Owen sank back in the bed. Grabbing his wrist in my left hand I felt for a pulse. He was still warm but his eyes were closed and his arm felt dead weight.

"I can't find a pulse!"

JJ hopped on to the bed and straddled Owen. He held

his nose and brought his mouth down. I took out my mobile and moved into the kitchen. All the time JJ was yelling.

"Wake up, Owen . . . Wake up, you fucker."

When I got back to the bedroom JJ was pumping Owen's chest. Owen was rocking up and down in the bed, his hand flung out over the side. I knew then he was dead and no amount of pounding and breathing was going to bring him back. I pulled JJ off him.

"No, JJ! Leave it . . . Stop it! . . . Stop!"

JJ fell off him and stood back. "He can't be . . . how . . . ?"

I took Owen's wrist once more but found nothing. I gathered in his arm and laid it on his chest, then stood back and put my arms around JJ. I didn't cry or anything and I didn't feel sad either. This was all happening in some dream time where I couldn't catch up with myself or my feelings. Sometime in the future I knew I was going to feel bad and go off food and sleep and spend the best part of myself crying. But that was another time, another life. Right at that moment all I felt was a sense of vague distant shame for not feeling more, for not feeling deeper.

I moved to pull the sheet over Owen. JJ pulled me back.

"No, Sarah, stay away from him."

Dr Ryan arrived a few minutes later and ordered us out of the room. He could have only been a few minutes in there when he came out and called an ambulance.

"What happened?" he asked. "What do you know?"

We told him what had happened. He asked us if Owen was taking anything, any substances. No. Owen had no interest in anything like that. There were no pills in the house either.

"Have you rung his mother?"

JJ stood up and wiped his eyes. "I'm going to tell her."

"Sit down, JJ. You're in no shape to go anywhere."

"I have to."

I don't know where he got the courage for that. He told me afterwards it was the hardest thing he'd ever done and I can well believe it. While we waited I answered a few more questions. I told Dr Ryan how Owen was in bad form the previous night, pining after Mary G and the argument with JJ. Listening to myself it sounded like it was something that had happened in another life instead of ten hours ago. Dr Ryan listened and drew some paperwork from his bag.

"He was fine when we left him. Young men don't just die in their sleep."

"There'll be an autopsy, we'll know more then."

JJ pulled up in the car then and Owen's mother jumped out. She was in the middle of the room before JJ had his feet on the tarmac. The sleeves of her T-shirt were rolled up to her shoulders and her hands were red. JJ told me later he'd found her in the kitchen up to her elbows at the sink. Now she stood in the middle of the room looking at me and Dr Ryan. She was turning a small circle around her like she expected someone to come up behind her and tap her on the shoulder.

"Owen?" she said. "Owen . . . ?"

Dr Ryan led her into the bedroom. He pulled the door behind him. I waited and listened. Behind me I heard this gulping sound. JJ was sitting at the table with his hands

76

clasped before him. The car keys were twined in his fingers
and his face was twisted in an effort to hold back the tears.

Owen was removed from Castlebar morgue the following
evening and taken to the funeral home in the town. The
whole parish turned out, queued from the gates all the way
up on to Cross Street. Cars double-parked all over the square
and knots of men stood on Morrison's Corner smoking and
shaking their heads in disbelief.

It was a beautiful summer's evening, a small breeze and
gold streaks in the sky out over the sea. We stood in line
with the rest of the mourners and a few of our friends. After
the immediate family had some time alone with him we filed
into the funeral home and stood over the coffin with our
hands joined and tried to say a prayer. Owen was wearing
a dark suit I'd never seen before, his hands clasped on his
chest. I stood over him and never said a word, not to myself
or to God or anyone else. I had no thoughts. Owen's parents
and aunts and uncles sat by the wall and we went and shook
hands with them and told them we were sorry for their loss
and then stepped outside and stood around crying and
hugging our friends.

The lads in the football team carried the coffin to the
church—it must have been half nine when it crossed the
square. Dad was on traffic duty that evening, holding up
those tourists passing through who must have thought it odd
that a whole town could come to a standstill on such a fine
summer's evening. I walked with JJ and sat beside him in
the middle of the church. He hadn't spoken since he'd seen
Owen in the coffin. I think it was only then that he fully

believed that Owen was dead, seeing him there all pale and his freckles grey under his skin.

There was a bigger crowd at the funeral the following day.[†] Owen's mother stood at the graveside clutching a wreath of flowers and Frank stood with his arm round her; it was hard to know whether he was comforting her or leaning on her for support. All that grief in his face, those bloodshot eyes—he must have aged twenty years in those couple of days. JJ stood back from them with two wreaths in his hands, one from himself and one from his classmates. The coffin was lowered into the ground and a decade of the rosary was said. Then the gravediggers moved in to cover the coffin. They don't fill in the graves here in this parish until everyone has left. The thinking is that it's too hard for the family hearing the stones clattering down on top of the timber; the gravediggers just lay timbers across the grave, pull a green tarpaulin over it and decorate it with wreaths and flowers. The mourners pay their respects and move off, leaving the immediate family to themselves.

JJ and I went to Thornton's afterwards and sat at a table. There were six or seven of us there, all friends. Everyone was nervous around JJ. He was off in some miserable world of his own. Those who spoke to him said it was like talking

---

[†] Pinpointing the exact moment when the whole *Somnos* project became a phenomena of religious fascination, commentators focus on the third weekend of July at the Wittness Rock Festival in the Phoenix Park. Before the headline act JJ O'Malley's face came up on the giant screen which formed the backdrop to the main stage. Held for a moment while the crowd cheered, the image slowly dissolved into the

to someone standing twenty feet away from you. With no sleep in two days his eyes were sunk in the back of his head. He drank two pints and got up to leave.

"I'm going home, Sarah, I need to lie down."

"I'll walk out with you." I was wary of leaving him on his own, I didn't know why exactly but I was afraid for him.

"No, I want to walk home alone. It's been a long day."

"Call tomorrow."

"I'll call sometime in the evening. I'm going to the grave tomorrow."

He didn't call the next day or the day after that. It was four days before I saw him again.

Three months later, at the inquest, the coroner returned a verdict of death by misadventure. Analysis of Owen's vitreous humour—the fluid in his eyeball—showed a blood alcohol concentrate of .45—ten points over the levels of surgical anaesthesia we were told. Sometime during the night, the alcohol in his system depressed his involuntary reflexes and respiratory failure resulted. Four pints of cider and a bottle of 50 percent proof liquor on an empty stomach will do that.

---

ongoing spike and wave tracings of his EEG. In front of the stage a section of the crowd raised their hands into the air and bowed down in the act of worship. In less time than it took to register, the gesture spread through the body of the crowd, synced to the chant, "We are not worthy, We are not worthy." Those with the presence of mind raised their mobile phones into the strobing light, sharing the moment with the absent.

And of course we got to thinking had one of us stayed with him that night he might have been saved . . . Then again he might not.

Commentators aver this was the turning point, the moment when the project decisively renounced its positivist remit and made common cause with a generation anxious to move beyond the cowl and candle, the dry ice and swirling snyths of those faux mysticisms which had replaced a discredited institutional faith. Professing to discern "a numinous moment, denatured and forensic," one commentator was moved to ask rhetorically, "Who is to say they are faking it."

GERARD FALLON

He'd argued his best friend to death, that's how he saw it then and that's how he still sees it if I know anything about him. You have to remember that once JJ got hold of an idea or an idea got hold of him he couldn't let it go. Time and again I saw that in the classroom. And of course the neater and more vivid the idea the harder JJ clung to it. The trouble with this particular idea was that it wasn't some piece of abstract theorising or speculation; this was an idea which struck to the very core of JJ, not just how he had lost his best friend but to his own life and who he was. Worst of all it was an idea which may have contained a small grain of truth . . .

He didn't come back to school at the end of that summer. Sarah told me how he'd suffered after Owen's death, how he had trouble sleeping and how he was thinking of getting counselling, about the antidepressants. Around the middle of October I called up to visit him, just to see if there was any chance of talking him round.[†]

[†] As if feeling short-changed by the media images and hard-copy representations, the subjects have now become part of the nation's dreamscape. More than one person has reported them drifting in on their REMs, turning up in those twitchy moments between sleep and wakefulness when we are especially vulnerable. Case histories paint similar

Anthony opened the door for me and told me to go through to the kitchen. JJ was sitting beside the range when I went in. The look on his face told me I was the last person in the world he wanted to see. My plan was for some small talk before I launched into my speech but his first words put me on the back foot straight away.

"No," he said, turning back to the television, "and pull the door after you."[†]

"How are you feeling?"

He looked long and hard at me. No, I wasn't going to leave that easily.

He sighed. "Do you want tea?"

"If you're making it."

He got up and went to the table. I'd never been in his house before but the kitchen struck me as just the type of place two men with no woman in their lives would put together over the years. Stifling warm it was, the range going full blast and a smell of cooking in the air. Nothing in the way of pictures or ornaments anywhere, just a pile of washing on the armchair and an old dresser full of glasses and plates against the far wall. A tiled floor and a pair of

---

scenarios: they come en masse, they are in this together, well-mannered guests careful not to abuse their hosts' hospitality. But there is an anxiety about them, something imploring in the way they just stand there. It is as if they want to tell us something but are unable to cross the divide between potentiality and action. And while it would be easy to put words in their mouths we should be mindful that, coming as they do from the realm of the undead, their providential message is likely to be pitched at a frequency beyond our hearing and more likely than not in a language we've never had a primer for.

[†] These screens and monitors, these imaging technologies and recursive information loops—what's aspired to here is a God's-eye view of

threadbare curtains. But for all that it looked clean even under the brightness of the fluorescent light.

"There's sugar and milk on the table," he said, handing me the mug. "No biscuits or cake, there's no sweet tooth in this house."

"People are asking for you, JJ," I said, stirring in the milk. "People are worried. How are you?"

"Don't start," he countered. "I'm never going back. That's all there is to it."

"Never say never, JJ. You've had a hard time but never say never. It's a big decision."

"I didn't make any decision," he said. "It's just the way it is."

"I don't follow."

The nine o'clock news came on the telly. JJ didn't turn up the sound.

"I used to be a news junkie," he said after a while. "First thing every morning I'd switch on two radios and the television—it used to drive himself daft. The paper as well before I went to school, it was as if I couldn't fix myself in the world without knowing what was going on in it. At night I used to sit up looking at the twenty-four-hour news channels, CNN, Sky, the whole lot. But now I don't get a paper or listen to any news. None of it makes sense any

---

the phenomena, from within and without, with all space-time dimensions comprehended in its view. Cupped in this hold, past, present and future, with all their shadings, have vectored here from all angles, stressing the ongoing present beyond its narrow linearity. The present perfect continuous is unable to encompass the exact parameters of the phenomena. What's needed here, among other things, is a new tense.

more. A revolution in my bedroom is a *coup d'état* when I reach the kitchen. One nation's campaign against terrorism is another's war of liberation. One analyst's market downturn is another's necessary correction and so on . . . Now I come into this room at night and switch on the encrypted channels and sit looking at the blank screen till I fall asleep. Sometimes I tune into the pay-per-view porn. That's how much sense it all makes to me now; nothing but snow on the screen and voices circling, preparing to fuck each other. Everything I thought I ever knew amounts to the same pile of shite. I know nothing any more. Everything I've read, all my ideas, the same pile of shite."

I'd often been left gasping in the wake of JJ's thinking but right then I felt he'd set new levels of incomprehension for me. Not for the first time I struggled to get a grasp.

"I'm flummoxed. How does all this tie into you not going back to school?"

"I'm starting work Monday," he said. "Seamus Mac has a lot of work on and he's short of hands."

"You mean the holiday homes."

"Yes."

"You're wasting your time. You should be back at school getting your head down. Owen would want you back, you know that."

"Owen would want to be alive," JJ said shortly. "That's what Owen would want."

"JJ, the loss of a friend is no small thing, everyone knows that, everyone sympathises. I'm not going to tell you I know how you feel but I am going to tell you that anger and confusion are common reactions. You're not the only one to lose a friend, you won't be the last."

He was looking at me like I'd come out with some rare idiocy. For all his brains there was never any arrogance in JJ. He was too impatient for that, too ready to believe he could learn from anyone, from any situation. That was one of the reasons he never pissed anyone off. Annoyed them, yes, but never pissed them off—there's a big difference. In any debate or argument he'd listen to what you had to say and hear you out. Only then would he dismantle your argument and in as gentle a way as possible. But right then he was looking at me like I was a rare idiot and I knew that little and all as I'd said I'd said too much. It was time to go; I wasn't going to make any more headway with him.

"Your mind is made up so. You're starting when?"

"Monday morning, I'll be glad to start something new. A change is as good as a rest as they say."

"I wish you luck. So does everyone else."

He showed me to the door and put on the light in the backyard. I swung round the car and wound down the window.

"Remember, if you think of changing your mind . . ."

". . . I'd have changed it long ago. Goodnight."

I wasn't too upset coming away from that visit—I thought there was some hope. The way I saw it JJ would spend the year labouring with Seamus McNally, up at the crack of dawn grafting away in the cold and rain. I couldn't see him sticking it, he'd be well sick of it after a year. He'd start missing his friends and his books and at the end of the year he'd come back and put his head down. Maybe he was right, a full year labouring, good physical work, might do him all the good in the world. Maybe it was just what he needed.

But I was wrong and not for the first time either. JJ didn't miss his friends or his books. And he didn't sicken of the work either . . .

ANTHONY O'MALLEY

He wasted those two years after Owen's death. Going off working like that, drinking himself stupid; he just turned in on himself and gave up on everything. If you ask me JJ's coma began the day after Owen died, over three years ago now, not three months as everyone thinks.

He started working for Seamus Mac sometime that October. Seamus had the contract for those holiday homes you see now below the town and he took JJ on as a labourer, navvying, the usual pick-and-shovel stuff. It killed me to see JJ doing that kind of work, all that ability going to waste. Anyone who's done their share of that graft knows how hard and thankless it is; out all day in wet and cold, coming home at night bone tired and covered in muck, barely able to put a bite to eat on for yourself. There's a lot of talk about the dignity of the working man but I'll bet no one with JJ's brains would have chosen to do what he did if they had the option.

I'd have the dinner ready for him when he came home in the evening. He'd sit there at the head of the table where you're sitting now in his socks and working clothes, barely able to lift the fork to his mouth he'd be that tired. In the first months of that job there was a real push on; half the houses had been sold off the plans and the tenants were due to move in the following Easter. Seamus's men were working long hours, ten hours a day, six days a week and in the beginning JJ wasn't fit for it—tending two block layers, he just wasn't strong enough. Sometimes he'd fall asleep at that table and many's a time I threw a blanket over him there on that chair beside the range. That's all he did those first few months, work and sleep and eat once in a while. He started to lose weight after a few weeks and his clothes began looking like they were a couple of sizes too big for him. I was worried about him, afraid his health was going to break down. But he got used to it, he got stronger, and as Seamus said to me himself he was as good a worker as ever he'd come across. Seamus thought a lot of him; he even tried to fix him up with an apprenticeship. He wanted JJ to take out his papers and serve time as an electrician or a plumber but JJ wouldn't hear of it, he preferred the graft, working away without thinking. I was glad JJ turned him down. Seamus meant well but I was a happy man when JJ said no. The last thing I wanted was JJ tying himself into a four-year apprenticeship; I still had hopes that he'd give up the work and go back to his books.

We tried to make the best of that first Christmas, the two of us. Myself and himself went out for a few pints a few nights but you could tell his heart wasn't in it. Just to see him standing there in the crowd, looking off into the distance, you could see the loneliness in him. He left Thornton's New Year's Night shortly after the new year was rung in. When I got home sometime around two o'clock the house was in darkness. I thought he was asleep but when I went

88

down the hall I heard him crying in his room. I left him to it; what could I say? He was glad when the Christmas was over and he was going back to work. And to tell the truth so was I.

You have to remember JJ lost more than a friend when Owen died. He lost his second family as well and the nearest thing he's ever had to a mother. No one ever thinks of that, no one really has an idea of just how much he lost. Things were never the same between himself and Maureen after Owen died. How could they be? Not that she blamed him for it or anything, not in so many words anyway, but there was an uneasiness between them which has never been talked through. I know Maureen feels the loss—not just the loss of her son but the loss of everything he brought with him into her life. And one of the things he brought with him was JJ. He was in their house every other day, he'd been there almost every day since his first day in this village. And sure when he was growing up he would walk in and out of the house and sit into the table like it was his own. But that all ended when Owen died. It was just too awkward, both for JJ and for Maureen. It was Frank who told me all this. Not a day goes by he said but Maureen goes over to the grave and speaks to Owen. And every day she sees JJ passing up the road on his way to and from work. Can you imagine how that must make her feel, that reminder going by her window day after day? It's no wonder you can't get her to talk about any of this. Frank says she'll hardly talk to himself much less a stranger like yourself. And I could be wrong but I don't think JJ has stood on the floor of that house since the day he gave her the news. What would he have to say to her, what words would he use? Frank is different though, always has been. It's not that he doesn't have his feelings or his loneliness but he's one of the few people who doesn't believe that JJ was in some way responsible for what happened. He said to me once, Anthony, he said, these things happen, they're laid out for us and there is not a damn thing you or I or anyone else can do about them. It doesn't make it easier or better but that's the way it is. We have to get on with it, you and me and Maureen and JJ. We have to get on with it and make the best of it. I told that to JJ one evening after he came in from work.

"Was he over?" He was sitting at the table in his socks, still in his working clothes.

"He helped me pen up those few cattle. I'm shipping them off tomorrow morning. He was asking for you, he hasn't seen you in a while."

"Did he say how Maureen was?"

"She's very lonely, she found Christmas very hard. They're glad it's over, they're both glad."

"I met her last week; she was coming out of Durkan's. I hadn't seen her in months. We stood in the doorway looking at each other and we didn't have a word to say between us. It was hard."

"No word at all?"

"We spoke for a few minutes, the weather and whatnot. Then we ran out of words and she started to cry. She told me to look after myself and moved off."

"That was something."

"I didn't expect it. I just stood there watching her walk away and I didn't have a thing to say to her."

"She knows how you feel."

"She knows more than me so."

"That's too deep for me, JJ. All I know is that if anyone understands it's Maureen Lally. You were lucky to have her in your life."

"That's not what I am saying."

"You should visit her."

"I'd like to but I don't know." He pushed his empty plate into the center of the table. It always made me feel better to see him eating.

"How is the work going?"

"Not too bad, I don't feel it so much now."

"I was afraid of that."

"We're not going to go into this again, are we?"

"Would there be any point?"

"No point at all."

"Those houses should be ready soon; Easter is coming in late this year. How many of them are rented out?"

"Six of them, most of them have been rented out since they were chalk marks on the ground."

"The last time I was down there they looked a long way from finished. No paving or kerbing or anything."

"That'll be the last to go in. They'll landscape it around the end of March. The first tenants will be here in the first weeks of April."

You see, in spite of what people think we got on well together. JJ wasn't always difficult. Sometimes talking to him like that it used to stop me in my tracks to think that this young man sitting opposite me was my son. Often I'd find myself thinking back to those years I spent working in London, working and drinking and having the craic but never with any serious prospects of settling down with a woman or having a family. Then I'd look across at JJ and see how he'd turned out, what a fine young fella he'd grown into and I could hardly believe it. I'd say people find it hard to believe that moments like this ever took place between us. It's not the kind of thing you see written in the papers. All that nonsense about him being confused and guilt-ridden—that's only half the story and I suppose it's the half people want to read about. But it's not the full story and don't go thinking it is. There's a lot more to JJ than anyone has ever come near. That's one of the reasons I wanted to talk about him, to show this other side of him. People know one side of him, or think they do, but this is the side I knew.[†]

[†] No less here than there but like the Divine equally present every-where, the subjects have now taken their place in the weak polytheism of contemporary celebrity. However, empty of all significance and con-tingent on silence and mindlessness, their fame is of an unusually pure sort. Lying beyond sin and atonement theirs is the apotheosis, the end refinement of that condition which is famous for being famous.

SARAH NEVIN

That old cliché, time passes so quickly. It was hard to believe two whole years had gone by since Owen's death. One minute you're standing over an open grave with a wreath in your hand, the next you're two years older and walking into an anniversary mass.

Normally there wouldn't be that many at morning mass in the middle of the week but people had remembered so there was about thirty or forty people in the church when we got there—a good crowd. JJ and I took our place near the back and just as we were sitting down Anthony came in and sat a few seats up from us. Owen's mother and father were over on the left. When the priest came out he said a few words and then offered up the mass for the memory of Owen Lally. That's when it happened. JJ told me when he heard those words—*the memory of Owen Lally*—it felt as if someone had reached in and pulled out his spine. The pain, he said, the sense of himself collapsing. It was the strangest thing, I actually felt him collapse beside me like some big stringed instrument coming undone. He leaned out over the seat in front of him, bracing himself with both hands, as pale as a sheet and breathing like he'd sprinted all the way from the house. He straightened up and pushed past me into the aisle.

Outside in the church grounds he lay over the wall and got sick, puking and puking and sobbing as he puked. I stood over him holding his shoulders, urging him to get it all up whatever it was. When he stopped puking he hunkered down beside the wall with his hand over his mouth. He was green in the face and shivering.

Old Jimmy McNeely came across to us. He put his hand on the wall.

"Is that lad all right, Soracha?"

"Jimmy. Yes, I think, just a bit off colour."

JJ stood up and drew his sleeve across his forehead. "I'm freezing," he said. "Hello, Jimmy."

"How're you feeling, JJ? You want to get that lad home to his bed, Soracha. I've seen ghosts with more colour than that."

"You're late, Jimmy; the priest is on the altar."

Jimmy laughed. "It makes no odds at my age. Can you manage, Soracha?"

"Thanks, Jimmy, I'm going to take him home."

I drove to our house and put him sitting at the table. JJ was still shivering in the heat of the kitchen and he needed both hands to bring the mug of tea to his mouth.

"You don't look good."

"I don't feel good; can I use your bed?"

He slept about an hour and when I went in to see him he was sitting up pulling on his T-shirt. Some of the colour had returned to his face.

"Lie in for a while, I'm still tired."[†]

He reached up and drew me down to his chest, put his arm around me and his hand up behind my head. That was always his way of holding me. It was a long time before he spoke.

"That man must be over eighty years old."

"Who?"

"Jimmy, Jimmy McNeely. You wouldn't think it to look at him. Eighty years old and he still cycles into town for his plug of tobacco and few pints."

"He's such a gentle soul. A pint of your finest red beer, Soracha, and a small Jameson. That's what he says whenever he comes in. Sits at the end of the bar and when he starts singing 'Paddies Green Shamrock Shore' you know then he's had enough."

"He told me once that he's cycled all the way to the moon and back. Forty years as a postman in this parish. Thirty-seven miles a day fifty weeks of the year. All the way to the moon and back as the crow flies he reckoned."

He was quiet for a long while and then he turned on his back.

"I never knew he was dead, Sarah. A full two years and

[†] How did we get this tired? When did this fatigue become so total? If the truth be told there is no drama here. Five men on the flat of their backs, sunk below the gag reflex and pupillary response, struggling to raise a delta wave . . . there is nothing to tell here.

But it is not so much that there is nothing happening here as that it has all happened before and elsewhere. Here in the realm of the undead things have been speeded up, fast-forwarded to the end. This is where denouements are spliced into the opening reel, plot twists straightened from the off, loose ends cut away in the prologue . . . This

I never knew. Can you believe that? How could I be so clueless, so stupid. If anyone had asked me I would have said yes, Owen is dead, my best friend, my brother, is dead and he's never coming back, I know that. But I didn't know it, Sarah, I didn't *really* know. It was only when the priest said those words, *the memory of Owen Lally*, that's when I knew. *The memory of Owen Lally.*"

"It's passed so quickly."

"I have this picture of him," he said, "this image. It's the same image that comes to me whenever I think of him but for the life of me I don't know where I got it from. It's a sunny morning, always Monday even though I don't know how I know that either. Owen is outside Kelly's shop with a bottle of Lucozade and a pint of milk in his hand. He's wearing jeans and T-shirt, his working clothes, and he stops to take a swig out of the bottle. He puts the carton of milk on the window sill behind him and stands there swigging away, wincing and thumping his chest as he swallows. Then he screws the cap back on the bottle and walks up the street to where the David Brown is parked outside the Bunowen. He swings her out on to the street and takes off out the Westport road. I don't know where I got that from, Sarah.

---

is where bad guys throw up their hands after the opening credits and take what's coming to them, where adventuresses come with transparent motives and where skeletons are routed from closets in the opening act . . . This is where love affairs, pallid for the want of sundering and tearful reconciliation, have cut straight to the inevitable disappointments and recriminations, where sex is wound on to post-coital depression, where killers never get into their serial stride because the first corpse, no matter how battered and seemingly senseless, always manages to hold on to incriminating forensic matter, where appellants

Owen must have done that a thousand times in his life but I can never remember seeing him do it. But it's still the clearest memory I have of him, something I've never actually seen him do. How can that be?"

We had the house to ourselves that evening so we pulled the table into the middle of the back garden and made something to eat. JJ had come round to himself a bit by then. He was looking healthier and hungrier.

"Twelve bicycles, Jimmy said, that's how many he got through on his journey to the moon."

"I spoke to him outside the graveyard the day Owen was buried. He was so lonely I couldn't believe it, an old man sobbing into a big white hanky like that. You'd think with all his years something like Owen's death would be easier to take."

JJ shook his head. "I think it only gets worse. When someone like Owen dies in a small place like this it's not just death you're talking about. This village didn't just lose one of its sons, it lost a part of its future. Owen was the type of fella this village has hopes for, it saw its future in him. He was an only son, he was going to stay at home and run the farm, probably build a new house . . . Another couple of

---

skip over mandatory setbacks in lower courts to ringing exculpatory verdicts in courts of appeal, where civic-minded explosions ring in prior warnings and coordinates to the authorities and emergency services, where car chases are paraphrased into the moment of collision with paramedics and metal workers already on standby and where, in spite of the digital meter counting down the days in the top right-hand corner of our screens, our dramatis personae, our action heroes, stay terminally locked in first positions.

years and his kids would be going to national school and Owen would be going to parent-teacher meetings. These are the things that ended in Owen's death and that's why an old man like Jimmy was crying. Owen's death yes, but the future also. People round here had their fingers crossed for the likes of Owen, they had hopes and dreams for him even if they didn't know they were hoping and dreaming. Someone like Owen is public property in a small place like this. You must feel that too, the way people look at us when we're out together."

"I know the way people look at us but I just thought it was young love and all that kind of thing."

"It's more than that, Sarah, people have their fingers crossed for us too. They remember what it was like here in the eighties and early nineties, how sons and daughters got scattered to the four winds and never came back. That still frightens them even if they don't know it."

"Have you ever thought of going back, JJ?"

I knew the moment I opened my mouth that I'd made a mistake. The look on his face, he honestly didn't know what I was talking about.

"Back where?"

I paused and drew a long breath; I wanted to know. "You know, back to where you came from, back to see, to find out."

This look of disbelief crossed his face. "Where has this come from all of a sudden?"

"I'm sorry I brought it up, I was just thinking out loud. But, you have to admit, it's the most obvious thing in the world. All your questions and searching, all your anger, I thought a time came for adopted kids when they needed to find out about their roots and their blood relatives. I'm sorry; I shouldn't have brought it up."

We had never broached this topic before and now that I had I wasn't sure I wanted to hear him talk about it. He laid down his fork and shook his head.

"It's a fair question, I've asked it myself more than once. But think about it, Sarah, what would I do if I went back? Look up registers and documentation? Find some poor woman in a tower block or rearing pigs on a small farm, a woman who has moved on with her life and who has probably forgotten all about me? Worse maybe, find out that she has died and that's all there is to it. No, I've never wanted that. I've never felt my roots lie anywhere other than here. This is my home, Sarah, these are my roots, this is where I belong. I might have come into the world a thousand miles away but that was before I was born. I was born here, Sarah, and I belong here, I've never felt any other way."

"But all those stories, all that talk about those other kids and the guilt, that's all part of you."

"It's too late to go back, Sarah, that's all in the past. Anything I found there would be out of place and out of time for me. All that anger and guilt, as you put it, has to find its answer here. This is my home, Sarah, don't go making me homesick on top of everything else."

"I just don't understand. You're now saying that all that happened before you were born and it has nothing to do with you. All you're saying is that you were born to be angry and guilty and bitching and moaning at the world."

"Maybe that's exactly what I'm saying. Things happen in your life and they make you what you are, but coming into the world is not one of them. Neither is dying. They're only bookends, they have nothing to do with your life. Think about Owen. Think about him. His death had nothing to do with his life."

"Nothing except end it," I said shortly. There was something here I couldn't understand and it was making me angry.

"Apart from ending it, it had nothing to do with his life whatsoever. It had a far greater impact on mine and yours."

"Jesus."

"I don't mean it like that."

"The worst sort of hair-splitting . . . I don't understand."

"What makes you think I do?" He picked up his fork. "Let's drop it, Sarah. This food is going cold."

KEVIN BARRET TD

Why JJ you ask? Let me say from the beginning that I am glad once and for all to go on record and clear up some of the misunderstandings which have arisen in the public mind over this project. A lot of confused nonsense has been written about it and I am glad of this chance to clarify things.[†]

Firstly, there was never any ulterior motive or agenda in choosing JJ. This idea that JJ's background, his adopted status, presented some sort of an easy option is wholly untrue. His background was not an issue. His application came through the same channels as the others and it was subject to the same evaluative process. This project was open to everyone. It was written up in the national press, you could go into any government office or library in the country and pick up an application form and the literature. Failing that you could download everything from the Net. It was all out in the open

---

[†] Legally, there were no insuperable obstacles to the project. Harmonisation of judicial and sentencing procedures across the EU meant that the smooth running of the project was down to making sure it didn't snag on translations of conveyancing warrants and so on. Documents had to be flawless. Months were spent haggling over them by translators and paralegal teams, calibrating every nuance and word before they were brought to effect. It's a tribute to the work of these people that each of these warrants passed without hitch through the relevant courts and legislative bodies.

and that was the way JJ's application came to this department. It arrived at department offices two days inside the deadline; you can see it here and you can see also the date of receipt stamped on it.

Secondly, JJ O'Malley is not a criminal. He has never served a prison sentence, never stood before the courts, nor are there any outstanding warrants against him. JJ O'Malley is an innocent man. That is important to stress because it is rumoured in some quarters that JJ is under suspicion for some crime or other. None of this is true so it is worth repeating: JJ O'Malley is an innocent man. No doubt confusion has arisen in some parts of the public mind because of the nature of the project. Yes, it is a penal experiment, it comes under the jurisdiction of the European Penal Commission and it is charged with research into the possibility of using deep coma as a future option in the EU prison system. And yes, it is true that four of the five participants on this experiment are serving sentences. JJ O'Malley, however, is not one of them. The reason for that is simple; it lies in the nature of the experiment itself. In any laboratory experiment of this kind conducted with multiple subjects over such a

---

There was no shortage of volunteers. Several countries—Germany and France in particular—were inundated with applications. Most of them came from prisoners serving long-term convictions with an eye to passing three months of their sentences as quickly as possible. Most were deemed unsuitable from the off. A screening process affixed to the European Penal Commission's initial proposal and further amended in consultation with various legal advisers significantly reduced the eligible number of volunteers. Serious offences, second offenders and likely recidivism excluded hundreds of applicants. These

timescale there has to be a control, a standard of comparison against which the re-actions of the others can be measured and compared. That is JJ's function on this project. As an innocent man with no prison record he is the control, the baseline reference, the norm. This is standard experimental procedure and it was the responsibility of this department to find such a control. Hence JJ.

Once we drew up a shortlist of those candidates who had passed through the physical and psychological tests, the choice came down to an interview and the two-hundred-word essay each volunteer submitted with his application. Speaking for myself this was the most tedious part of the whole process. Almost without exception each essay exceeded the word limit. This in itself was sufficient grounds for binning them; however, we persevered. In general most of the essays were nothing more than a hotchpotch of clichés and second-hand platitudes—furthering the glory of science, to do something for my fellow man and so on and so forth. After reading a handful of them I felt as if I was judging a beauty contest. I half expected one of them to say they wanted to travel the world and work with handicapped kids. But JJ's effort stood out. Two hundred words was the limit; he submitted twelve. *I want to take my mind off my mind for a while.* That's all

---

amendments were the first obstacles within the internal constitution of the project. The EPC worried that the amended screening process would prove overly restrictive and narrow down the pool of volunteers below a viable threshold. They were out of sympathy with the concerns of the legal bodies. However, the legal advisers would not countenance any circumvention of justice and, as one of them said in an internal memorandum, "If the twin concerns of justice and research could not be conjoined then the project had no future." This focused

he wrote, *I want to take my mind off my mind . . .* You can imagine after so many screeds of cliché and platitude how sudden and direct this was. It spoke to the heart of the issue and unlike the other scripts it spoke clearly and directly. It cut through all the dross and verbiage and spoke more in twelve words than the rest did in two hundred words or two hundred pages. The immediate impression it gave was of a clear mind which was direct, highly intelligent and with a merciful ability to spare words—a mind which did not beat around the bush. This was what it said to the panel, the five lay readers. Of course this gut reaction was not enough; we could not proceed on the basis of our layman's analysis. To support the panel each application was handed over for evaluation to the forensic psychologist at Castlerea Prison, Jane Evers. Each script was handed over as a numbered file, with only relevant biographical details like age attached, but no names or any other details. The only stricture placed on Evers was that her report be written with as little technical jargon as possible—it had to be accessible to a general audience. This is her report:

Totalling a mere twelve words, the brevity of the text prevents us from subjecting it to any of those intra-

---

minds and a joint session of both bodies published an agreed document which contained all the proposed amendments of the legal advisers within the EPC's initial conditions. Legally and medically, each volunteer would have to meet each condition separately and independent of each other; there could be no question of an aggregate success.

It was essential from the point of view of public confidence that the project be seen to come under the authority of the EU penal system. This was to offset worries that research institutes might gain

document analytics which enable us to compute those fault and readability indices which accommodate conclusions about the writer's educational level; the lack of complex words using suffixes and prefixes is a further prevention. Likewise the absence of recurring phrasal patterns, adjectives, adverbs and intensifiers preclude conclusions as to the writer's state of mind vis-à-vis such moods as stress, anger, anxiety, etc. Given the context and its intended audience one might surmise that the note was written in this abrupt manner with just such a purpose in mind.

Without mood signifiers and devoid of any circumstantial evidence concerning the writer's life and loved ones the text might therefore be better understood as an elliptic philosophical argument. Expressed as a desire, the writer wishes to have his mind escape his mind. Implicit here is a distinction between his mind and the intentionality of his mind—his thoughts. His wish to relieve his mind from the stuff of his thinking, be they experience, memories or ideas, points to a kind of dualism which can be interpreted as a wish to achieve a peace of mind independent of thinking. While recognising that his thinking is a defining part of his identity as a conscious being, the writer now

---

a foothold within the EU penal system which would allow them to come in and recruit volunteers for further projects. To guard against this, a redundancy clause written into the project's constitution would come into effect at its close.

In line with this, the governor of the *Somnos* would have ultimate say on when and if the project should be aborted. A full-time medical observer liaised with the attending neurosurgeon and anaesthetist on a daily basis

believes it to be a process which is damaging and which, for a while, he seeks to be relieved of. His thinking is now other, an unintegrated and mendacious part of himself. One might say that the writer is at odds with his own thoughts and seeks for the time being to be rid of them.

In this context the writer's temporal orientation is of interest. Entered as a qualifier which accepts the limited duration of the experiment the phrase "for a while" implies acknowledgement of a future wherein the writer sees himself ready to resume his cognitive selfhood once more.

It should be noted that nothing in the text indicates a suicidal or parasuicidal ideation. The text evinces none of the hostile or exculpatory themes common in suicide notes; if anything its brevity and refusal to enter any justifying arguments points to a mood of fatigue. Neither does the writer levy any of the usual value judgements on himself or on loved ones. The self-reflexiveness of the text prevents the writer from seeing himself as a social or cultural being; nowhere is the self considered as perceived of or thought of by others. The subtlety and directness with which it addresses the question is also at variance with the emotive and repetitive rhetoric of suicidal

_____

and so long as his report squared with the daily report of the project coordinator the project could continue. Any discrepancy between these reports or deterioration in any of the subjects' conditions below certain paremeters would be taken as legitimate grounds to abort. Ultimately, next of kin retained an absolute right to withdraw the volunteers at any time.

discourse. Nowhere is the word "love" or its many synonyms used. Constrained within their narrow theme and stressful context, suicides show little ability to think about thinking and seldom if ever achieve the subtlety of this note's embedded argument. Suicides and parasuicides do not make good philosophers.

Written within the context of the experiment the script's severe brevity presupposes a large degree of background and contextual information on the part of the reader. This is a deliberate application—we can assume it is carefully pitched to arouse curiosity and an aura of mystery. Nevertheless, the writer's clarity of mind and disinterest in the project as a whole are attributes which should strongly recommend him to the panel.

As you can see, Evers' report expands somewhat on our layman's analysis, more or less confirming in academic language what our hunch told us. That was heartening but we needed more. The next stage was the interview. JJ was one of five who'd made it through to this stage but it was still anybody's guess as to who would be successful. Walking into the room he made an immediate impression. We were familiar with his background from his file but his height and his cheekbones took some of us aback; he was more Slavic-looking than Latin. And there was this confidence about him as well. Straight off it was obvious there would be no attempt to glad-hand us or second-guess what we wanted to hear. Yes, he had read the terms and constitution of the project, but no, he had no interest in it. Whether it was successful or not as a penal experiment did not bother him. Yes, it was a historic opportunity, but no, he assured us, he had no wish to make a name for himself. Yes, he had discussed it with his loved ones and, no, it hadn't been easy. However, his father was used to this degree of recklessness in his personality and if he did not exactly have his enthusiastic blessing he was here with his best wishes. Of course he anticipated a degree of media curiosity about whoever was chosen and yes he was prepared to do a number of interviews. However, beyond the fact that he was a fit young man with the necessary degree of courage, he didn't see that his personal biography was all that relevant. This was an important point and it was well answered. The other candidates had come across far too eager to fill out the blank spaces of what we knew would be one of the stories of the year. JJ's wariness struck a different note. It spoke the proper sense of his role in the whole thing and when, as we anticipated, the whole project became a media circus this was the type of diffidence we needed in our candidate. Finally, what was in it for him? A rest, he said simply. To go to sleep for a few months, nothing on his mind: just a rest. The impression he gave during all of this was that he was doing us a favour. His demeanour was that of a man with other options on his plate and the loss would be ours if we did not choose him. It was arrogance all right but it was the kind of arrogance you could warm to; it inspired confidence. He spoke clearly, without rambling. No, he had no questions of his own, everything was clear to him and it was the shortest of the five interviews. Watching him walk out of that room my feeling was that we'd found our candidate.

I wasn't the only one with this feeling. A straw poll around the table after the interviews showed him to be the favourite. He was elected by a unanimous vote at the next meeting and he was informed a few days later and told to report for a medical briefing in Beaumont Hospital. Of course the interview and the psychologist's report were not the only deciding factors. JJ is a single man—that was important; no spouse or dependants were part of the criteria. Also his physical condition—two years working as a labourer had left JJ fitter than most men his age. His cardiovascular fitness and fat to muscle ratio were the best of all the applicants. Odd as it may seem coma patients need their bodies to sustain them. Muscular atrophy is an inevitable effect of long-term coma no matter how much physiotherapy they receive. But according to medical projections JJ had muscle to spare— two years shovelling and pushing wheelbarrows had seen to that.

That, loosely, was the procedure and evaluation process. You can read a more detailed account of the whole thing on the official website. This is a public experiment and most of the material can be accessed by the public. The only information kept private is the family details and the individual medical histories of the candidates. And of course it's JJ's medical history which has you here today. Let me say that the disclosure of this information is a severe embarrassment to this department. A full public apology has been issued to JJ and his loved ones and how it became public was the focus of a departmental inquiry. Unfortunately, the inquiry never reached any conclusions. Lines of inquiry just disappeared into the sand. When his medical history was lodged in the official website guest book we were appalled. That attachment was traced to a public library in Dublin where the email account was set up. The account had never been used before nor has it been used since. That is as far as any back-trace can go. That is the difficulty of the Web, its openness and anonymity.[†]

Of course that disclosure cast a shadow over JJ's involvement. Yes, we knew of his medical history and it was discussed by the panel. But it was not considered an obstacle. JJ was not ill, mentally or physically, when he was chosen. When he presented for the project he was ten months out of St Theresa's with a clean bill of health. The confusion about JJ's state of mind arises as a result of all those articles which persist in confusing unhappiness with mental illness. They are not the same thing, as any psychologist will tell you. Put simply, a person who is unhappy or sad or guilty or grieving is not necessarily a sick person. Sadness is not an illness, neither is guilt or grief; it does not have a pathology despite what all the New Age spoofers would have you believe. Whatever about being desirable it is a normal part of the human condition. And to say, as some have, that JJ was not in his

---

[†] Is this how we faded from ourselves, the protein and electrical weave of the self giving up the ghost and watching as it drifted away, with good reason, through these walls? And did we part on good terms, shake hands and go our separate ways but still, in our heart of hearts, hanging on in the expectation of a plaintive call or a postcard from the other side telling us we were missed, *wish you were here . . . ?* Or was it bitter and acrimonious, both of us glad to be shut of each other, both of us vowing never again, not in this life?

Something in the here and now disappoints us, something in it has us turning away from it. We might say that the time and place is gone

110

right mind is pure arrogance. JJ's right mind is a sad mind—that is his normal condition. That is not the same as saying that his condition was desirable but it is the fact of his whole existence. He is not a happy young man. We knew all this and it was explained to us by the supervising psychologist. We discussed it but did not see a problem.

And that's it; those are the reasons and that was the process. I can assure you it's all above board—certainly no other project in the history of this government or any other has gone through such an exacting series of checks and examinations. Medics, lawyers, accountants, environmentalists—all areas of expertise were considered. The Attorney General was consulted to make sure nothing in the project would offend the constitution—the Council of State was convened twice. The world is looking on at this, everything has to be out in the open. This project will not be filed under conspiracy in some sort of paranoid *X-Files* dossier. It's about figures, nothing more or less: the punitive cost of the present-day prison service. And yes, I have an investment in all this. This is my constituency; JJ is one of my

---

when we were identical with ourselves, when we were at one with our IDs and no margins or discrepancies threatened our ontic alignment. Now, by way of imaging technologies, information systems and bureaucracies, we find ourselves in this lateral drift from ourselves. Nothing else can account for this rush towards the abstract. We have come to live in this deferral of ourselves, drifting away on a digital tide, a hail of ones and zeroes which sift down through the ether and resolve to a lattice of pixels on screens and printouts—our very own hauntology. We have renounced the here and now, drifted to elsewhere and elsewhen, trailing in our wake a spoor of forensics and telemetry over a paraphrase of our timelines, a line of crumbs we hope one day to find our way back home over.

constituents. I have to go before the people in two years' time for re-election; the last thing I want is to be writing letters of condolences to loved ones and answering questions before a government subcommittee. Something going wrong is not an option.

SARAH NEVIN

A couple of weeks after that incident in the church we had our first real argument, our first lovers' tiff. The weather had taken up and I suggested we go away together for a few days, just a week or so on our own to get some sun on our pale faces: the kind of thing lovers do, I didn't think it was too much to ask. Of course looking back now what I was really trying to do was move our relationship on to another level. We'd been a couple about three years by then but we'd never been away together, never spent any time alone together, so one week in August seemed to be just the thing. JJ had holidays coming and I had some money put by; I couldn't see a problem.

But JJ wouldn't hear of it. He wasn't being awkward or anything but the idea just struck a fear into him I had never seen before. He put his foot down, a blank refusal; it was as if I'd asked him to up sticks and move away altogether. That shocked me because it was the first time he'd ever refused me anything. As a rule he was only too happy to do anything to please me, anything to put a smile on my face as he put it himself. It was just the way he was. All the care and attention he'd lavished on me at the beginning of our relationship hadn't tapered off in the least. He'd kept it up effortlessly. Three years had shown me that it was more than

the rush of attention you'd normally expect at the beginning of a relationship. All the presents and gestures, the
courtesy and attention—he was a real romantic.

But this idea of going away together was different. He
wouldn't even discuss it.

"No, Sarah, let's not get into this. I don't want to go anywhere."

"It would only be for a few days, JJ, some sun and sand,
waking up together. Just some time to ourselves."

"You've been planning this?"

"Don't be paranoid; it's a suggestion not a plot. We could
go anywhere."

"I'm not going anywhere. You go, get someone else to go
with you."

"I don't want to go with someone else. This is about you
and me. Let's get a map and stick a pin in it, do something
reckless. We have the time and the money, a few days away—
we could forget about things for a while."

"No."

"What are you afraid of? This is what lovers do. It would
be such fun."

"I'm not afraid of anything, go yourself, I don't want to
hear anything more about it."

And that was the end of that discussion.

So my idea came to nothing. I was so angry I threw a huff
and went away with a friend—ten days driving around
France. It was good fun but towards the end I was glad to
be getting back. By then of course I'd cooled down and for-
given him. All I wanted was to see him and show off my

new tan. But when I got back I found that everything had gone to hell.

First thing in the door Mam tells me he's in hospital.

"I tried to contact you but your mobile was out."

"When did he go in?"

"Five days ago, Thursday afternoon."

"An accident? What happened?"

Mam blanched and looked down at the ground.

"No, Sarah . . . he's in St Theresa's."

"He's not a well man, Sarah," Anthony said when I drove over to the house. "He's not a well man at all."

Whatever about JJ, Anthony looked ghastly. If I hadn't known I might have thought he was the one who was sick. He stood there in the middle of the kitchen, no shave and the hair standing out on the side of his head as if the fright of the last few days was still thrilling through his system. My own sudden appearance had upset him also. He kept tugging at the cuff of his shirt and looking around the kitchen as if he'd misplaced something. The curtains hadn't been drawn; the kitchen was filled with this orange murky light. A mess of stale dinner things lay on the table and the chairs were covered with clothes and papers; in just five days the bachelor had broken out in Anthony.

"The trouble with that fella, Sarah, is that he's too smart for his own good. Too smart entirely."

"I'm going over now, Anthony. Can I bring him anything?"

JJ's bedroom was where he spent most of his time reading and listening to music. Unlike the kitchen it was perfectly tidy: his books and CDs on one wall and his bed against another, the wardrobe built into the wall opposite. Whenever I went into it I always had the feeling I was entering a monk's cell. No posters or pictures or anything on the walls, just the bare necessities. This was the kind of impression JJ strove towards. He had this idea that if your bedroom was tidy then your life was tidy also. That was why he decluttered every couple of months or so, sorted out all his old clothes and letters and anything he didn't need. He'd gather the whole lot up in a black bag and light a fire against the gable of the shed and stand over it till it burned away. It always made him feel better he said, gave him the impression of moving on, turning over a new leaf.

Anthony put a few things into a bag, underwear and T-shirts and so on. I pushed in his Walkman and a handful of CDs. Anthony handed me the bag.

"When you see him, Sarah, don't be too shocked. He's not a well man."

He was in St Anthony's ward, sharing a room with five other patients. An old man with a wide grin on his face sat propped up on a pillow by the window. Opposite him a young man was turned face to the wall clutching a small radio to his ear. JJ was sitting on the side of his bed in his own clothes—jeans and T-shirt and a pair of toeless sandals. They were his clothes all right but they didn't seem to fit. Hanging limply, drooping and creased, they looked as if they'd died the moment he'd pulled them on. No light in his eyes or colour in his face and his hair swept over to one side of his head, like a little boy going up to his first Holy Communion. This more than anything upset me. He looked so lost in himself; there in body but his mind a million miles away.[†] I sat down beside him and took his hand.

"How do you feel?" I seemed to be asking that a lot lately.

"How do I look? Tell me how I look?"

"You look lost, pale and lost."

"That bad?"

"No, you're awake, that's a good thing."

He was looking at me intently, scanning my whole face. A gust of breath shuddered through him. He placed his hands on his knees to steady himself.

"Sarah," he blurted. "That's it . . . Sarah." Tears shone in his eyes. "Christ, it was touch and go there for a moment, I was really scrabbling. What's happened, Sarah . . . ? Tell me what's happened."

"Can you not remember anything?"

"This is my first day awake. Everything's a blank. Doctors won't tell me anything. Tell me." He squeezed my hand. "Please."

"Maybe we should leave this to the doctors."

"No, Sarah . . . Please."

Of course he had to know. This was JJ, what else did I

[†] Truth is, the soul of man under womb-to-tomb surveillance has not revealed itself. Try as we might we have yet to raise the ghost out of the machine. Still fleet of foot and ever fading beyond whatever probes and spells we have to hand it has yet to be drawn out into the light where we might hear it give an account of itself. Mapping the cortical and subcortical regions of the brain, tagging the neural correlates— none of this has brought us any closer than a distant telemetry which refuses to arc across the meat to mental gulf . . .

expect? After a moment thinking about it I felt it would be better coming from me than someone else.

"You'd gone to work—or so Anthony thought. But when he got home that evening he saw your boots and jacket in the hall so he knew you were still in the house. When there was no sign of you for the dinner he went to your room and found you sitting on the side of the bed, naked and blue with the cold. Your whole face had collapsed in on itself he said, this grey colour, it looked like porridge. You didn't speak or move or recognise him and you were as stiff as a board—like a man who'd spent the whole day doing press-ups he said. He pushed you back on the bed and threw a blanket over you and then called the doctor. The doctor spent five minutes with you and then told Anthony he was getting an ambulance to take you here. A nervous breakdown, he said. Anthony sat with you till the ambulance came but he couldn't get a word out of you. When they brought you over here they sedated you and gave you a muscle relaxant. Anthony came to see you last night but you were asleep. He's been here every day since you were brought in."

And that ghost and host might be integrated beyond the wildest complexities of quantum causality, cottered in some way beyond the crude ecumenics of mentalism and physicalism, forces the idea of considering the ghost to be one of those basic universal elements like space and time, fleeting and irreducible, unspeakable in any terms other than its own. Or that the ghost-in-itself might not just in practice but in principle also lie beyond all epistemic probing, fenced off by a self-reflexive short circuit; or that beyond semantic fuzziness it may be nothing of any substance at all—these are the boundaries within which we hope to grasp it.

"Anthony who?"

My heart lurched. I tried to wipe any expression from my face.

"Anthony's your dad; you'll see him later this evening. What's the last thing you remember?"

A long moment passed.

"The last thing before you came here?"

He narrowed his eyes and shook his head gently as if clearing his thoughts.

"I was at mass, I got sick. When did that happen?"

"Over three weeks ago."

"What happened in between?"

"You went to work as you always do. We were supposed to go on holidays but we had a fight and I went on my own. I was gone ten days."

"Do we fight often?"

"No, not often. You're awkward but not one for fighting as such."

"I have this feeling . . . so feeble, like I'm strung out all over the place. Why do I feel that?"

"You need rest, JJ, you need to build yourself up."

I've never seen anyone so lost to himself, so distanced from his own strengths and energies. It wasn't so much that

_____

Our best hope is that one day the ghost might tire of the chase, take pity on our awkward fumblings and give itself up. One day we might round a corner and find it waiting for us with a look of amused sympathy on its face. *What kept you?* it might ask or more likely *How exactly did you get this far?* But of course there is every chance that, awkward to the last, anything it has to say for itself will probably be spoken of in a language which flies over our heads.

he was disoriented or lost to the world, it was more like he'd drained away into some hole within himself and had left only this shell behind him. There beside me within arm's reach, but the best part of him a million miles away. Was he seeing me at the same distance? I wondered. Was I as far away from him as he was from me?

"You're going to get a lot of rest and sleep, JJ. You need it. You've been through a lot this last year."

He drew my hand to his cheek. I wondered who'd shaved him.

"I need help, Sarah, I don't know what's happening to me. I sleep from one end of the day to the other, but waking or sleeping I can't suffer myself. That's all I know, I can't suffer myself."

We talked some more and I left him after an hour, promising to return the following day. To tell the truth I was glad to get out of the ward—the smell, those squeaky floors. At the nurses' station I caught up with the specialist in charge and after a few minutes trying to get through to him that yes, I was his girlfriend, he told me that JJ had suffered a mental breakdown, a stress-related check of his psyche. The serious aspect of it was that part of his memory was occluded—his declarative memory, the long-term memory which deals with learned facts and narrative.

"It's not unusual," the specialist said breezily, "this retrograde amnesia. In this kind of breakdown there is generally some degree of memory loss and disorientation. But it's not a calamity. It will return. The good news is that his procedural memory is intact—he showered and shaved himself this morning. That is a good sign. He will need rest and sleep for a few days and then we can go about rebuilding him. Don't look so worried. Whatever's wrong with him he's in the best place for it."

Outside, a big yellow sun hung in the sky. Leafy trees cast shadows over the car park. It was the type of summer's evening you made plans for, swims and walks and quiet drinks. But there I was standing in the car park of a mental hospital with a lump in my throat and my boyfriend inside bludgeoned with sedatives. And all I could think about was what that doctor had said about him being in the best place. The thing was that the best place for him was worse than anything I could ever have imagined.

ANTHONY O'MALLEY

Of course it's easy with hindsight to say we should have read the signs, the writing on the wall as he'd have put it himself. But if the writing on the wall said something about a mental breakdown before the age of twenty then it took keener eyes than mine to read it.

I used to go over to him in the afternoon—I had it arranged with Sarah that she would do the evening shift. Those first few days visiting him were penance, not just for me but for him also. He spent most of his time sleeping and during those times he was awake he could remember nothing; his memory was gone. His doctor explained to me that this was not unusual in breakdowns of this type. There were therapies and exercises and medication and with time and rest he could hope to make a full recovery. It was a relief to hear that but I have to say I didn't have much hope for him during those first few days. Seeing him in that ward, so clueless and bewildered, it was like meeting him again for the first time as an infant—an infant dropped into a twenty-year-old body. Back again in his own childhood but with no idea that it was his. Bit by bit though he did come back to himself and one afternoon when I went over he was pulling on his shirt getting ready to walk out for cigarettes.

"Let's walk together," he said. "A walk would be good."

The shop was two hundred yards away, just beyond the roundabout. JJ looked pale in the sunlight, paler behind a pair of black shades. But I thought by the way he walked that something of his old self was returning to him. It was good to be out in the air as well, anything was better than wandering through those corridors. As we walked I was struck by the fact that this was the first time in years we had walked anywhere together. It's the truth—once father and son reach a certain age they literally go their separate ways.

"They're pulling back on my medication," he said, lighting a cigarette. "Seemingly I'm fit enough now to sleep on my own."

"That's good news."

"They're starting this evening, tonight will be my first night without pills."

"That'll help the other thing . . . your memory. Is anything coming back?"

"Bits and pieces. Let's sit here for a while."

The bench was under a big sycamore in a shady part of the front lawn. It faced on to the main road off the car park, in full view of the roundabout.

"I have this image of myself reading a book," he began. "Or rather I'm reading the inside cover of a book. This same image over and over. *This book belongs to JJ O'Malley, Cahir, Louisburgh, Co Mayo, Ireland, Europe, The Earth, The Milky Way System, The Universe, The World.* That's all I have . . ."[†]

_____

[†] His name scrolled out to infinity invokes a lonely image—the intrepid space child, thumb in mouth, adrift among the stars with nothing

What else but a book, I thought. Books before everything.

"Do you know what it means?"

"Yes, I remember it clearly. When you went to school you were a bit younger than your classmates and when it came time for the class to make its first Holy Communion there was some talk of holding you back and having you make it the following year. I put the foot down; you were smart enough and good enough and I didn't want you falling behind in anything or getting separated from your friends. After some talk Eileen Mangan—she was your teacher at the time—said it was fine by her. She agreed with me; you were smart enough and good enough, there was no reason why you should be kept behind. You were given this little catechism, *The Light of Christ*, and you put your name on the inside cover. That's the book you're on about."

JJ shook his head. "It means nothing to me."

"It meant everything to you at the time. It contained all the questions and answers you had to learn off in preparation for the big day. Who made the world . . . that was the first one."

"God made the world," JJ replied automatically.

"Yes, and who is God?"

"God is Our Father in Heaven."[†]

---

save his first catechism to guide him home to this imaginative standpoint. As an early attempt at self-definition the child's claim to locate himself against the limitless reaches of the heavens prefigures the technological phenomena of image and information dispersal which characterises the *Somnos* project.

[†] Considered as a mystical state, one of those privileged moments

"See, you remember more than you think. Those were the first two questions in the book and you had it all off. Every evening you'd sit on the couch and I'd examine you on it, question after question. Within a few days you had the whole thing memorised from front to back. It was the first real inkling I had of just how smart you really were—it was the first inkling Eileen Mangan had as well. She called me up a few days after you got the book and I could tell by her voice she was worried. So smart she said, the smartest child I've ever taught. But the questions you were coming out with! The topic of original sin—you couldn't leave it alone. What exactly was Adam's sin?—even then you weren't buying that orchard-raiding story. How was the sin transferred down to us from Adam? Was it the sin itself or was it just the guilt that was transferred? Was it like vertical transmission of disease in livestock? Bar the Virgin was anyone else exempt from it? How could a merciful God allow this? What exactly was aggravated concupiscence? Day after day you harped on it, putting her to the pin of her collar till she was forced to go out and spend ten pounds on the big single-volume *Catechism of the Catholic Church* just so that she could stay ahead of you. He's a gifted child, she said. There's no doubt about that. But I wouldn't care to have his ideas in my head. Not at six years old—or sixty either."

---

when God steps forward out of His primordial loneliness to take a bow, coma may be one of those vortices through which God is freed into the universe. Having written Himself into the world not as an idea but as an emergent property of neuronal activity in the superior parietal lobe, a signature accessed through suppression of all stimulus which orients and delimits us in time and space, it may be that these

"And that was my book?"

"That was your book."

"Where is it now?"

"Burned . . . probably. You're a great burner of things."

"I remember, that I do remember. Aggravated concupiscence . . . what the hell is that?"

I shrugged. "You'll have to ask a smarter man than me."

"I'll ask Sarah. I'll make a note of it."

"Do that. Sarah might know right enough."

This was my part in his recovery, talking him back to himself. He'd get these flashes, these dreams and images, sometimes in his sleep or sometimes just walking about. He'd make a note of them and have them ready for me when I went over. I'd read through them and tell him what I knew about them. Of course if you ask me he might have been better off forgetting some of them completely. But they were his memories and I had no right keeping them from him. So we'd sit on that bench under the tree and I'd tell him what I knew.

I handed him back his notebook.

"We have to back up a bit for this one. Around the time you got your catechism you found out you were adopted. You came home from school one day, your face red raw from crying. You dumped your bag and coat on the floor

_____

selfless God-bearers have lain themselves open to His immanence . . . through the vortices of these open minds God comes among us as pure potential, something prior to His Father, Son and Holy Ghost visitations, a phenomenon rarefied beyond the validating ecstasies of mystics, meditants and temporal-lobe epileptics.

and told me that you'd had a fight in school. Someone had called you a name and told you I wasn't your real dad and that your home wasn't your real home. You were trying to be brave about it, your two fists balled up on your hips, biting your lip to stop crying. I put you up on my knee and tried to explain it to you. I told you how I had travelled halfway round the world to find you in that orphanage and how I had the pick of thousands of other little boys but that none were as nice or as special as you. And I told you also that some mothers weren't able to look after their little boys; in fact, it was because they loved their little boys so much that they had decided to hand them over to these orphanages. That was as good as I could do for you that day. But of course it wasn't enough. You sat on the couch that evening and no amount of coaxing would get you to move from it. No, you didn't want to go and play with Owen, and no, you didn't care what you had for dinner. You grew up before my eyes that evening, JJ. Something solemn entered your soul."

"It doesn't explain the image of me lying in a room with a drip in my arm."

I drew a deep breath. "Some things are so awful, JJ, you can't look them square in the face and some things make no sense no matter what angle you look at them from. And of course they happen in other people's lives, never in your own."

"These are my memories, Anthony. I need them. I mightn't want them but without them I'm nothing."

"I know . . . About two weeks after that you were lying in the children's ward of the general hospital with this drip in your arm; I was down the hall sitting across the desk from a child psychologist who was telling me that in twenty-two years of clinical practice she had never come across a child suicide attempt before. She's read about them but never come across one before. Of course the first thing out of my mind was to deny it.

"'No,' I said, fearing I was going to lose my temper, bang the table and barge out of the room. "It was an accident. JJ didn't know what he was doing."

"'That's what I thought, but after talking to him I know better. Sit down, Mr O'Malley . . . please."

"I hadn't realised I'd risen from the chair.

"'JJ has a rationale and, frankly, had I not heard it myself I would not have believed it.' She waved a sheaf of papers at me. 'JJ is an exceptional child, you know that. I have his SAT results here and I have never come across anything like them. At six years of age JJ has the reasoning capacity of someone two and half times his age. Right now there are students studying for their leaving who do not have half his brains.'

"'I know how gifted he is. That doesn't mean he tried to kill himself.'

"'On its own, of course not, but above and beyond JJ's logical capacity he has this ability to draw ideas together, to make connections between them and draw inferences and conclusions from them. That's not unusual in itself, it's the way children learn about themselves and their position in the world. But JJ's ability goes way beyond that, he has the ability to see these things as part of his own life and existence. More than that he takes them to heart.'

"'This isn't telling me anything,' I blurted. 'How does it explain him lying there with a bellyful of rhubarb leaves?'

"'Two things have come together in JJ's mind over the last few weeks. Firstly, the fact of his being abandoned to the orphanage. That came as a shock to him and that is to be expected. Usually we advise that children be told this kind of thing when they are on the verge of puberty. They are better able to cope with it. With any luck the years of care and love they've had up to that point will stand to them. They should be secure enough in the parental environment to cope with it.'

"'JJ didn't have that luxury.'

"'Yes, he told me and no one is to blame. However, the second thing: JJ has been studying hard for his first Holy Communion and he has become fixated on the doctrine of original sin. JJ has put these two ideas together, his abandonment to the orphanage and the doctrine of original sin, and he's come up with a quite extraordinary narrative.'

"'Narrative?'

"'Story. His abandonment to the orphanage and the doctrine of original sin have come together in his mind and created the conviction that he is guilty of some unspeakable sin. He sees himself as without grace, graceless.' She looked down at the desk and sifted through her papers. 'Mr O'Malley, most people will go through their entire lives without ever reaching this kind of existential self-awareness. Most people can live quite happily without it. Those who cannot, some of them, have seen fit to write long impenetrable books on the subject. For anyone it is a considerable intellectual achievement but for a child it is well nigh beyond belief.'

"'And that was why he tried to kill himself, this guilt thing?'

"'No,' she replied. 'JJ wasn't trying to kill himself—he was trying to save himself. *I was trying to go to heaven*, he said, those were his words. In his religious instruction he has learned that children live in a privileged innocence and if they die in this innocence they will go straight to heaven.'

"'I'm confused, the child is either guilty or innocent. He cannot be both at the same time.'

"She nodded. 'I had to look this up and I find that JJ's reasoning is a bit garbled but it is not entirely incorrect. On one hand Catholic doctrine teaches the idea of original sin, this guilt from which no one is exempt. On the other it tells us that up to a certain age children exist in a state of innocence, essentially blameless and without moral responsibility. But come a certain age they are thought to possess reason and as a result know the difference between right and wrong— moral responsibility. That age is roughly thought to be around seven years old. It is not an arbitrary cut-off point. Children of that age show accelerated signs of rational and deductional powers. Their personalities become shaped, they become capable of reasoned decisions; in some jurisdictions they can testify in a court of law. For JJ this is hugely significant . . . Yesterday we had a small party for him. A nice little cake and seven candles. He blew them out and then burst into tears. When I asked him what was wrong he said it was now too late. It took me a while to make the connection—JJ was telling me it is now too late to commit suicide.'

"I remember sitting there for a long time repeating that line to myself; *it is now too late.* That was the sort of thing that passed for good news in those days. After a long moment I asked her if she believed all of this. She spread her hands.

"'Mr O'Malley, I would believe anything this child told me. I have never met anyone like him. I don't expect to meet anyone like him again.'

"By then I badly wanted to get out of the room, my head was swimming and my throat was dry. I rose to go but she hadn't finished.

"'One last thing. He said as well that he was sorry . . .'"

"'That's a start,' I said, grateful. 'That's a good thing.'

"She shook her head. 'That's a bad thing. What he meant was that he was sorry he was born.'"†

Those were the type of memories I found painful going back over, memories I could well have done without myself. But of course they were exactly the type of thing JJ needed to know about himself. Sometimes though the mood between us was lighter. He'd come upon other stuff that was just plain daft, of no real importance in itself other than that it was the stuff of his life.

---

† Spooling through his head these cross-fades and dissolves, the memory wipes and flashbacks of this self-generating narrative. Splicing together the threads of himself, aligning these twitchy structures which throw him out of sequence with himself, these longeurs which give him pause. Linear and sequential, beginnings, middles and ends in

He raised his face and pointed under his chin. "This scar. How many fights did I get into?"

I guffawed, relieved to talk about something daft.

"Nine stitches and a tetanus jab, it wasn't a fight. Four years ago you came into my room at four o'clock in the morning, covered in blood. You'd been in a car accident. Coming out of Skamps you'd taken a lift home with the Shevlin twins—they'd just bought their first car—a ten-year-old Toyota. Out over the bridge, foot to the floor and the music blaring—you were sitting in the back. Somewhere along the way a row broke out between the lads in front—was the Toyota a two litre or a one point eight. Whatever it was it hadn't brakes enough to keep it on the road at the turn above the factory. Straight into the field it ploughed, turned over three or four times and it was the grace of God you were all able to walk away from it. Coming across the field in the dark you tripped and cut yourself on a length of barbed wire in the grass. You got a tetanus jab later that morning."

"The Shevlin twins, who're they?"

"Two of your buddies. You went to school with them. They're in Boston now. Null and Void."

"Null and Void . . . who put that on them?"

"You were the first I heard with it."

"Jesus."

_____

their proper places—this is what is needed here. It's as if the whole project could come into being only as an image of the very structure and process it now serves to suspend—every breakdown and reversal, every distraction, false start, list and seemingly pointless excursus having at one time its correlate in the process of consciousness itself.

"They're good lads but not the sharpest knives in the drawer. But that's the way you are, JJ. You see these things."

SARAH NEVIN

Whenever I've tried to bring him to mind these past three months it's always the same picture that comes to me: the pale JJ on that bench under the tree looking at me with this clueless expression on his face, his pupils dilated like black suns. You'd think after all our time together I'd have something else to draw on. It just shows though how powerful and odd those weeks were.

"We have the time," I said, "we can build you."

"Rebuild," he corrected tonelessly.

"Is there anyone else in the room with you?"

He shook his head. "No, it's a small room, just a desk and a chair. Once in a while this man comes in and takes away the finished sheet on my desk. He lays down another and walks out. The sheet is always the same, multiple-choice questions and puzzles—if two typists type two pages in two minutes how many will it take to type eighteen pages in six minutes. I'm flying through them but it makes no sense . . . Do you know anything about it?"

"Yes, I remember it, the myth of the boy genius was minted in that room . . . You were six years old when our teacher Eileen Mangan sprung a surprise exam on you— the Scholastic Aptitude Test—the entrance exam for the Irish Centre for Talented Youth in DCU, a test of mathematical and verbal reasoning. You sat the exam alone in her office; it took the whole morning. Six weeks later the results came back; the youngest candidate ever to sit the exam and you'd scored eleven points over the entry threshold. Your IQ put you in the top 1 percent. They offered you a scholarship, wanted to take you on that summer."

"So I went off to this infant hothouse?"

"No. At the time the institute was an eight-week summer camp. The choice was up to you but you weren't interested. Even then you weren't keen on travelling."

"So now you tell me I'm this genius with not a thought in his head?"

"It won't always be like that."

He took the disc out of his Discman and passed it to me, a blank home-made compilation. "This disc, Sarah, all these torch songs and schmaltzy ballads . . . You can't convince me I've ever had a taste for this kind of stuff."

"You'd have to take my word, wouldn't you?"

"Right now it's all I have."

I saw the initials on the disc. "SN," I said. "Sarah Nevin. This is mine, you must have made a copy of it. This is the first thing you ever gave me after my car accident."

"You as well?"

"Car crashes are a right of passage thing for our generation—broken bones and stitches, our badges of honour. I came to it a bit younger than most, a few years ago now. It wasn't too serious but I did crack my head and spend a week unconscious. You came to see me and the second time you came you had this compilation for me. You'd asked around, found my favourite songs and downloaded them on to this disc. A comfort disc, that's what they're called in the ICU community.† I was wired up to it for a couple of hours a day. It's supposed to stimulate the auditory cortex, part of the ongoing stimulus therapy. They think it might have some effect in recovering people from deep coma . . ."

"And that's how we met?"

"Yes. You bluffed your way on to the ward, told the duty nurse you were family. When you saw me swathed in bandages and hooked up to those machines you fell in love with me. A sleeping princess you said, and all those

---

† . . . mainly private messages and greetings from loved ones, each subject's private "listening" is confined to one hour a day. However, the ship's sound system random-selects through this small library of aural stimulus and comes up with some startling and downright dissonant conjunctions. At any moment Shostakovich's Seventh Symphony might, without dropping a phrase, be rooted in the opening chords of "Reign in Blood." Maria Callas finds herself back to back with Patti Smith, whales and Cistercian monks call out in their separate frequencies, the Folsom prison recordings segue into Hildegard of Bingen, New Age relaxation tapes of woodland sounds meld into Ennio Morricone soundtracks which in turn give away to a selection of Scottish mining songs . . . Pairing the music with its contributing volunteer has become a lively game on the official and unofficial chat sites. Some pairings are obvious. Luftig's background draws in all the heavy metal, probably also the *Sturm und Drang* of Wagner, Orf and Beethoven. Gainsborough and Emile Perec are an obvious pairing. Online friends confirm JJ's weakness for Hank Williams, the Smiths, Leonard Cohen— anyone who has sublimated self-pity to an art form. Scottish mining songs and the collected works of Ewan MacColl are easily accounted for, so too the dance rhythms of Underworld and Fluke. But what of all the devotional music? Who is responsible for Byrd's *Mass for Four Voices*, Allegri's *Miserere*? Did whoever volunteered Pärt's *Tabula Rasa* hope to refine further its ache towards silence in Cage's *4'33"*?

136

vigilant machines agonising on my behalf . . . I had to be special."[†]

"I really am sick."

"It wasn't your fault. I threw myself at you—threw myself at you insofar as it's possible for anyone in a coma to throw themselves at anyone."

"It's not exactly textbook grounds on which to start a relationship."

"I had to be original. You were one of the school heroes, the one with all the looks and the brains; I was just another of the plain Janes mooning at you from a distance. There was no reason why you should have noticed me and were it not for my accident you never would have. But I'd nearly

---

Baffling as the musical soundtrack may be, it is a paradigm of narrative coherence compared to the spoken-word pieces which have found their way into the mix. Randomness and whim and downright historical mischief are the narrative imperatives here . . . Malcolm X vows by any means necessary and Desmond O'Malley pledges to stand by the republic. Galileo betrays himself to the Inquisition and 365 years later in Havana, Castro commends John Paul II on the posthumous pardon. Luther draws a line in the sand and says here I stand, I can go no further; Satan, down but not out, determines to make the best of a bad job but Lucifer, his sidekick, does not fancy the odds. Robert Shaw attests there is nothing deader than a shark's eyes; John Doe tells us that only in a world this shitty could these people be considered innocent . . . And so on and so on . . .

While within the hold fiction and history are put through narrative loops beyond all unravelling, there are those optimists who speculate that in spite of appearances there might be some truth unfolding here, some tireless heuristic at work which might at any moment resolve the larger narrative into some previously unsuspected coherence above and beyond the immediate determinism of historical cause and effect . . .

[†] As good as any place, a place where dissent festers. Here in the

137

died in that car crash—nearly but not quite—and that was something you respected. For all your brains and reading I had direct experience of something you had only ever theorised about. That gave me allure and it got your attention. It was good enough to start with. Sooner or later your heart would follow."

"And it did?"

"It did."

And that's how it was with us during those days, how we put him back together, piece by piece, Anthony and myself leading him into the dark places of his mind and switching on the lights for him so that he could find his way back to himself. What amazed me most was how

---

sacral quietness of the ICU, the architectonics of man-machine symbiosis is reaching its apotheosis. With pain and systolic drudgery already contracted out to these machines, leaving these subject/object hybrids in their wake, the machines continue dreaming their machine dreams: a world without obsolescence or wear and tear, a place where optimum functioning is a way of being—dreams of redemption, what else? The worry is, however, that some day we're going to get the bill for all this. One morning we'll walk into our kitchens and workplaces and find a list of demands nailed to the door: kettles and fridges and domestic appliances petitioning for various constitutional amendments, universal suffrage, round-table talks on a minimum-wage agreement; these vigilant machines, worn out dreaming us, agonising on our behalf, appending protocols for counselling and compassionate leave; cars filing sexual-harassment suits; public lighting systems and the national grid drawing up the terms of productivity deals; the Internet, gathering in all its constituencies under one banner and making a case for full statehood before the UN General Assembly. Because, in the dead of night, and with the human flowing from us into these machines, who is to know that this is not happening? The least we can do is have it straight in our minds how we're going to greet him, our brother in Christ, Robo sapiens. Are we going to turn our backs

easily the world can become fragmented not just in one person but also in the lives of those about them; that someone's life was such a fragile weave of connections and interlocking stories was news to me. One of the first things I realised was that I was not only telling him his story but mine also. Recovering myself in his mind was now part of my job as well. I had to make sure that I too was not lost in him otherwise something about me would remain only half a story and that, as JJ would say, was no story at all. So I became anxious over and beyond my concern for him. Each day, just to prepare myself, I'd try second-guessing what he might say, reaching to get a head start on him. But I'd let him choose whatever he wanted to talk about, I took the lead from whatever fragment came to him during the night and nagged him. He used to say that he could feel these parts of himself crying out to him for telling. All the scattered pieces of himself . . .

In other circumstances it would have been fun, a couple reliving old times insofar as a couple our age had old times. But now it was mostly an anxious job of work—love and sentiment had little to do with it. We were reconstructing a person. And incredibly, piece by separate piece, we did bring him together. Each little story drew another into the light and each in its turn reached out and formed other connections, bringing bigger parts of his memory into life. JJ was fascinated by the process.

---

on him and give him the cold shoulder? Are we going to say, "Hail fellow well met"? Or, in this moment of recognition, will we put out our hand and say, "It's good to see you, son, what kept you?"

"Rebuilding myself," he said. "Yourself and Anthony the hired labour. A few more weeks of this and I'll be able to stand back and admire the whole thing. Hopefully the whole thing will come in on schedule and under budget."

But of course there were lapses, awful dead ends where he remained stuck for days, dark cul-de-sacs he could find no way out of. Some of them were even comical.

"Of course you can't separate them. They're identical twins, no one can separate them."

"Null is Paul's brother," he repeated, "the older of the two."

"Yes, and Paul is the one you worked with."

"Null and Void, the Shevlin twins. They were in class with us but they left for Boston over a year ago?"

"Yes."

"And I put that on them?"

I shrugged. "It's not far from the truth."

"And they're my friends."

"Yes, you worked with Paul on the holiday homes. He was one of the block layers you tended. You drank with him in Thornton's after work."

"So why would I go putting that on them? Am I that big of a bollox?"

"It's the way you are, JJ, you have a way with words."

"Jesus," he said grimly, shaking his head.

Anthony and I took it in turns together, divided the day into two shifts. If I did the afternoon Anthony made sure to be there in the evening. We never talked about it as such or drew up any plan, it just happened that way. JJ just pointed out to us where he wanted to go and insofar as we

140

knew the way we led him there. Sometimes he didn't want to talk so we'd just sit together on that bench holding hands, plugged into his Discman and listening to whatever piece of music had taken his fancy that particular day. Like his reading, JJ's choice of music was all over the place. That was another of those things about JJ, something which could wrongfoot all his friends. One minute he'd be wired up to some Norwegian death metal, the next he'd be humming along to the rawest of the raw *sean nós*. No rhyme or reason as he said himself. But there was one piece he returned to again and again on that bench. Arvo Pärt's *Tabula Rasa*. If there is a soundtrack to those days when he was groping towards himself it's that twenty-five-minute piece. JJ bought it for me shortly after we became an item. It was a bit of a statement—he loved the piece, he used to lie in his room with the light off smoking and listening to it; giving it to me was a statement of his feelings towards me. He was telling me that I was special. It's one of the ways we came together, hooked into those circular phrases, orbiting round each other in a world above and beyond ourselves. Hearing it for the first time I thought it was the most beautiful thing I'd ever heard. It sucked me in, the beauty and sadness of it, its aching towards silence. But now I can't stand it. The backs of my hands start to itch in the opening phrases and I'm back on that bench in the hospital grounds with no sunshine or anyone else in the world but ourselves. And those phrases, circling round each other and moving towards that empty fade-out . . . I feel myself sinking and breathless within them now. But this was the piece JJ came back to whenever he was stuck for something to talk about.

"It's not that I understand it," he said, "it's just that I like the sound of it. Some days I'm a complete blank. I feel like an astronaut floating around inside myself, no coordinates or direction, no clue which way is back or forward. Sometimes I feel I might run out of air and choke in the absence of myself. That's why I play this piece. Circling round itself and inching forward towards its own completion, that's all I can bear sometimes. Aching towards resolution but dying on its own feet."

ANTHONY O'MALLEY

He was discharged towards the end of May and, as he put it himself, came home to Louisburgh for the second time in his life. He had no plans to go back to work, no plans at all, and that suited me fine. If hanging around the house for the last few months of the summer was what he needed to gather his wits and strength about him then that was OK with me.

He was like a pale giant that evening standing in the kitchen, his thin face and narrow shoulders, his wrists sticking out beyond the cuffs of his shirt. For some reason I thought he was going to strick his head off the fluorescent light over his head and bring the whole thing down around his shoulders.

"Either you've grown or this ceiling has dropped."

He reached up on his toes and tapped the fluorescent with two fingers. It stopped flickering, a steady light fell.

"That's hospital food; everyone should have a spell of it."

He dropped his bag and shoved it to the wall with the tip of his boot. "It's good to be home," he said, "you wouldn't believe how good." That was said for both of us and it was good hearing it.

After we had a bite to eat he sat back and looked around him like he was seeing the room for the first time.

"A lick of paint wouldn't go astray on these walls," he said. "When was the last time we took a brush to them?"

"Two bachelors, what do you expect? There are a couple of cans of emulsion in the shed, enough to do this room and ceiling. I suppose we could take a look tomorrow."

So we did—or rather he did. The following morning he stood in the shed looking at the dribs and drabs in the bottom of the paint cans.

"Magnolia," he said, pressing the lids back down. "There must be other colours in the world."

He jumped in the car and was gone about an hour. When he returned the back seat was full of cans and a new roller. These colours you see here on these walls and throughout the house are all his work from those days. I suppose a change was what he wanted and this was what he came up with. It was the same throughout the house, the halls and the bedrooms; he changed the colour of everything. He did the outside too, the plinth and reveals, changed the colour of those as well. He must have spent the best part of two hundred euros on paint and of course he wouldn't let me put my hand in my pocket. No, he said, I'll do this myself. I knew then this was his way of taking his mind off himself and of course he threw himself into it the way he did everything. There was never any half-measures about JJ. It was as much as I could do to get him to take a break and put a bite of food in his mouth at dinner time or in the evening. I was afraid he would suffer some sort of a relapse so I used to go into his room at night and take the clock from beside the bed and let him sleep on into the afternoon so he could get some real rest. Of course he knew well what I was doing but he never said anything.

Frank called over to see him after a few days. He stood in the kitchen looking around him, passing the palm of his hand up and down the wall.

"God bless the work, JJ, you're busy."[†]

"Frank, good to see you."

"Any man doing all this must be in the full of his health."

"I feel fine, it's good to be out of that place."

"I'll bet. It's an awful dose."

"You wouldn't wish it on anyone."

"There's some who would. You'll do the outside as well, I suppose?"

"Might as well now that I've started."

Frank nodded. "You might as well. Will he raise any hand to it himself?"

I motioned Frank to a chair. "I would if I was let, Frank, but he has to do it all himself, there's no talking to him."

"You're right, JJ. Old fellas like that are more hindrance than help."

Frank always had this soft spot for JJ. It was never anything he did or said about him, it was all in the way he talked to him—like he was his equal or like they had something between them that only they knew. Whatever it was it always gladdened me to see them standing around

---

[†] The smooth commencement of the project met a hitch one month before the green light. From his prison cell in Stockholm Haakan Luftig requested clarification from the EPC as to the volunteers' status while the project was operational. What seemed a simple enough request was complicated by Luftig referencing various articles of EU law which governed the rights of EU workers with regards to wages and conditions. His point was obvious. Since the volunteers were contracted to the EPC for the duration of the project they were de facto workers

together talking as if nothing had ever happened. That was Frank's doing. After Owen's death he did his grieving and got on with it and tried his damnedest not to let any bad feeling grow between our two houses. Without him things would have been a lot worse. Life is too short for bad feeling, he told me a few months after Owen was buried. You don't get over these things but you learn to get around them. Move on, make the best of it. Anything else is a sin against life.

That was the first time I'd ever heard that and it made me wonder how many of us are guilty of that kind of sin.

"If there's anything I hate it's painting," Frank said. "I leave it up to herself, it only leads to arguments."

"There's no arguments here. JJ's doing it himself, that's all there is to it."

"There's no rush, leave something for tomorrow. The man who made time made plenty of it."

You could see JJ was satisfied the evening he finished. He put the cans and rollers in the shed and stood out at the gate wiping his hands on a rag.

"It's a bit brighter anyway," he said. "We should have done it a long time ago."

"It makes everything else look bad," I said. "We should

_____

and therefore came under EU guidelines for remuneration and conditions; their worker status entitled them to a day's wage for what Luftig was now insisting was a day's work. While the request was immediately interpreted as an attempt on Luftig's part to embarrass the Commission it did raise a valid point; if the Commission conceded the subjects' worker status then the 168-hour working week contravened all existing labour laws. One member of the Commission was so irked as to ask whether any subject in deep coma could meaningfully be

throw out some of that old stuff; it takes the look off your work."

He shook his head. "It's fine," he said. "It's just the idea."

Of course when he'd finished painting he was left with nothing but time on his hands. What was he going to do with himself then? There was no talk of going back to work nor did I want to hear any of it but JJ was never a man to sit around doing nothing. The first thing he did was pull the table and chair from his bedroom out into the yard and set up a sort of desk there. That's where he sat most of his days, eating and reading, smoking and drinking water out of a plastic bottle.

He was lucky the weather was so fine, blue skies every day and the yard lit with the sun reflecting off the white walls. They were the type of days that open your eyes to just how beautiful it is around here—something that's easy to lose sight of during the winter months when the sky is down on the ground and the wind cuts in from the sea. But when the sun is shining and those hills are out from under the clouds you wouldn't wish to be anywhere else in the world. We're lucky up here on this height. On a clear day you can see up to Lachta in one direction and out to Clare

said to be engaged in anything which might accurately be described as work—wasn't consciousness a defining precondition of human labour? There followed a debate within the Commission which, after two hours, had progressed little beyond a provisional definition of terms when Magnus Dubois, Professor of Medical Ethics at the École Normale Supérieure, drew a line under the discussion. The issue, he said, was not one of conditions or remuneration but of Luftig's intent to draw the Commission into an abstract and faintly ridiculous debate

Island in the other—the only thing between ourselves and America. If you take a walk into the fields you have a clear view all the way up to Inishturk; with a blue sky over your head you wouldn't believe the world could be so big. When we worked together in London, Frank told me this was one of the things he missed about this place—this openness, this sense of space. Of course at the time I didn't know what he was talking about—I've never had a feel for these things. But some days now I walk out and I begin to understand a little clearer what he was on about.

You wouldn't think it but JJ made a good convalescent. He read outside and took his meals at the table and didn't move to turn his hand to anything about the place. I was glad of that. By that time the silage was wrapped and the few loads of turf we needed for the winter were in the shed; all the heavy work was done. But, knowing JJ, if he had wanted something to do he would have found something. He didn't. He just sat there and soaked up the sun and it was only when I saw him with a book in his hand that I remembered I hadn't seen him reading in the longest time. Again, it was only a small thing, but it made me happy to see him doing something like that. I would have been happier still if he had given up the fags. That was

which would do nothing but damage public perception of the project and position Luftig himself as the volunteers' spokesman. If the project was to have any future this must be avoided at all cost. As for the definition of work and the worker status of the volunteers while in coma—this was precisely the sort of philosophical havering Luftig was counting on to draw down ridicule on the project. Dubois concluded that rather than draw out any discussions and run the risk of having the debate go public, Luftig should be encouraged to put his

something I worried about. I jarred him about it one evening at the table.

"Mark my words those things are doing you no good."

He smiled and tossed the match into the ashtray. "This was the first thing I remembered after I woke up—the fact that I smoked. I never knew I was that fond of them."

"All I'm saying is that you have to look after yourself. The only other man to smoke in this house was my father, your grandfather, old Tom, as everyone called him. I knew he was dead the night he stopped smoking."

"I thought he died in his sleep."

"He died in his bed whatever about his sleep. He was never a good sleeper. He'd wake in the middle of the night and smoke one fag before turning over to get a few hours before morning. He'd have it rolled on the table beside him so he could reach out and find it in the dark. I used to go up to him every morning with a cup of tea. That morning I went up the first thing I saw was the fag; it hadn't been smoked. I didn't even look at him; I pulled the door behind me and drove into town. As luck would have it Mattie was crossing the square as I pulled up. I told him the craic and he said not to worry, he'd take care of it. I had three quiet pints in Conlon's on my own and when I got back Mattie had him laid out, candles and flowers and everything."

---

demands on paper immediately. A meeting in Stockholm was arranged. Luftig's initial demand was that each subject be paid the minimum wage for each and every hour of his coma. The Commission refused to be drawn into a tacit admission of a 168-hour working week and countered with an offer of a minimum wage over a thirty-eight-hour five-day week with double time at weekends for the duration of each

"But he lived to a big age."

"He might have lived to a bigger age if he hadn't smoked. All I'm saying, JJ, is that you have to look after yourself." The sun had dipped behind Clare Island and there was a sharp chill in the evening. "Are you not cold sitting here? There's a heavy dew falling, the grass is covered in the morning."

"I'm going downtown in a while. Sarah is working. I'm going to have a few pints in the hotel. Are you going down?"

"I was thinking of it. You'll be in the hotel so?"

"Yah. I'll be there till she gets off. Call in, a few of the lads will be there. There's a game on the box."

"Maybe."

"Do. Sarah will be glad to see you."

So I did go down and I was glad after. I had two pints with JJ, two quiet contemplative pints as he put it himself, and Sarah stood me another at the end of the night when she came outside the bar.

---

volunteer's coma. Luftig played hard to get a further five days then signed a contract to that effect, confirming the impression that his point was not one of principle or gain but a calculated attempt to mark out a pre-eminent position for himself among the volunteers. The other subjects were given similar contracts, bank accounts were opened and the incident served to make the Commission more vigilant.

SARAH NEVIN

So how then did it come to this? How did he go from con-
valescing in the sun to lying on the broad of his back out
on that prison ship? If you'd seen him during those days
you'd have seen a young man on the mend, someone who
was sensibly looking after himself, gathering his strength
up there on top of that hill. There was something about
him during those days I'd never seen before, something I
liked but which made me rethink a lot of what I thought
I knew about him. This stillness came over him, he barely
moved. From the bed to the kitchen to the backyard, by
and large that was the extent of his world. It was like he
was tethered there within some boundary visible only to
himself and beyond which he was loath to stray. His
strength was going to converge on that spot and he had to
be there to gather it in when it returned. But he was a joy
to be with during those days, more attentive towards me
than he'd ever been. Learning to cook was one of the things
he did with this time. Before that he'd never shown any
interest in food but now, with time on his hands, he began
doing things with woks and shellfish and artichokes. He
was in two minds about this new skill and I teased him
about it.

"It will be happy for the woman who gets you," I used to

say whenever he made me sit down to eat some new meal he'd prepared.

"It's a sure sign of a man with too much time on his hands," he'd reply. "A man with no proper work to go to."

After we'd eaten we'd go and lie down in his room for an hour or two, draw the curtains and make love in the green light which played across his bed . . .[†] All this made me hopeful. Lying in each other's arms I thought we were home and dry, coming into the finishing straight of a bad time. The future didn't exactly come into focus for me there in that green light but I could have sworn there were blue skies and sunshine hanging over it.[‡] Of course I never guessed that all that stillness was part of the thing that was beginning to haunt him.

"This dream," he said one day, "I keep having this odd dream."

"They're all odd, that's why they're called dreams. No use asking me about them."

"Do you have a recurring dream?"

"Yes, as it happens, I do. I had this dream once as a child, a flu fever thing. I'm very small and vulnerable in it. I'm standing alone and naked in the middle of this open

---

[†] Three weeks into the project, Nielsen/NetRatings confirmed that "coma" overtook "sex" as the entry of choice in the nation's Web search engines. Only once before has this ever happened—during the second Iraqi conflict when "war" became the dominant search tag. What does this signify? What promises are being held out to us here? What exactly do we find so desirable? Why do we keep coming back here, day after day, night after night, to flick through the pages of this twenty-four-hour upskirt?

[‡] The weather in the hold is a simulation. Feeding off a continuous

---

space. Out of the distance these balls come bouncing towards me, big balls about three times my size, brown and soft like inflated internal organs, horrible things. All I know is that I can't let them touch me—for some reason I know that will prove fatal. So I spend the whole of that dream dodging and weaving, getting weaker and weaker . . . Not a nice dream. It comes back to me sometimes, not very often. I'm always seven years old in it. Don't ask me what it's about. Why?"

He rose above me on one elbow, his face in shadow.

"I can feel myself getting better, Sarah, becoming whole again. Day by day I'm recovering more and more of my memory. There's this thing in neurology, Hebbian linkage it's called. Basically, it states that neurons firing in the cortex set off chain reactions in neighbouring neurons which build up associative webs throughout the brain and integrate the whole of human experience. Basically, this is the mind-making process although how this neurochemical fizzing and popping results in consciousness is something I can't understand. None of the mind/body arguments I've ever come across make any sense to me.[†] But I see something

---

stream of data from the Carnsore weather station the full-spectrum light waxes and wanes through the moods of a day two degrees south of these latitudes. The delay in the transmission has the simulation lagging ten seconds behind the real thing. Save for Spenco boots and loincloths the subjects sleep naked. The lumens fall on their skin, duping their cellular chemistry into the ceaseless synthesising of vitamin D—like hothouse skinflowers. They breathe on under the unblinking gaze of registering monitors, within the vigilance of resuscitative machines.

[†] In the second year of his administration and seven months after the fall of the Conducator, the leader of the free world set his hand to

similar happening with my memory. One memory sets off another, linkages and connections are established, people and places and events are falling into place and I can recognise more and more of my past self. Except for one thing. This dream I've been having—I can't place it, it just doesn't fit . . . I'm lying on a bed in a dark room, dead tired and unable to move. It feels like I'm drowning in that dark room but there is no way I can move away. There's this crippling pain in my left leg which won't let me get off the bed. And I'm falling asleep, this dense sleep is moving in on me. I'm terrified, it's not like any fear I've ever known. I don't want to fall asleep but I can't prevent it. I can't stop it moving in on me. At the very last moment, just when I'm going to go under, I wake up sweating and frightened. The strangest thing is that I feel fine after it— no pain or fear. I put on the light and look at myself in the mirror. And this is strange too—this feeling of having to wait a few moments before I catch up with myself. Like the real part of myself is still back in that dream. Does that mean anything, Sarah?"

"Are you alone, in the dream I mean?"

---

designating the coming decade the "Decade of the Brain." The resulting House Joint Resolution 174 ushered in a decade of funding and research comparable to that prompted by the 1958 National Aeronautics and Space Act.

Scrying with advanced neuro-imaging techniques and with various meat to mental dependence theories as working hypotheses, a generation of neuro specialists turned inward to map a universe of such depth and complexity that by comparison the probings of the various *Apollo* missions were but local tourism. Somewhere within the clints and grikes of this new world glittered the real prize: consciousness.

154

"Yes, I'm all alone—that's one of the terrible things about it. I have this feeling that if someone comes in and talks to me I will be OK."

"How come you can't get off the bed?"

"I'm tired, tired and nauseous. There's also this pain in my knee."

I could have walked away then, made some excuse and gone home and got my thoughts together. If I had wanted that badly enough I could have got up and walked away. But I knew these things and he didn't.

"This is a need-to-know thing, Sarah. You're the one with the memories, my memories . . . and I have to know."

I knew that and he knew that I knew that. So I told him.

Afterwards he sat on the side of the bed, elbows on his knees.

"So you're telling me I have a detailed memory of something that isn't mine, something that never happened to me. Time and place and character where they should be but none of it mine."

_____

One result of the congressional imprimatur was a shift in the balance of funding and prestige from cardiac and oncological research to neurology in clinical institutes. Neurologic facilities became the holy of holies within the clinical research community. Theoreticians of all persuasions crossed disciplines into a delicate nexus of technological probing and pure conjecture, a place of infinitesimal margins and staggering magnitudes, a knotty realm where connections dissolved before they were fully traced and gave way to ever more vertiginous speculation.

What at first glance appeared a heroic scientific enterprise had, in fact, its origins in an economic imperative. Fearing the rising cost of

"I'm just telling you what it looks like."

"How close were we?"

"Close as, closer than, brothers. But for appearances anyone might have thought you really were. You sat together in the same desk throughout your school years. Wherever one of you went the other was always a few paces behind. You even had this trick of sitting together reading out of the same book."

"Nothing odd about that."

"No, not reading, but turning the page without consulting each other, that was odd. Don't worry though, you were often seen together in the same room, there really were two of you."

"So I can hardly remember my own life but I have a detailed memory of my friend's death. My best friend, this crisis apparition, come back to haunt me."

"You had a hard time after he died—you gave yourself a hard time. If only I'd stayed with him that night, if only we had gone straight home, if only, if only, if only . . . Then you tumbled to the idea that you'd argued him to death—that didn't help either."

---

neurogenetic diseases, degenerative disorders, strokes, autism, depression and head traumae across an ageing population, heads of industry and insurance companies lobbied Congress for a federal and multidisciplinary investigation of the brain and, as an afterthought, the very nature of consciousness itself. The whole project was predicated on suspicion of the individual as a potential economic liability. This rationale turns on its head the Conducator's economic reasoning which earmarked a whole generation of neonates as fiscal assets whose life mission would be to drive up economic production and help redress the national debt.

"What's it trying to say to me?"

"It's part of what brought on this breakdown, a type of delayed reaction the specialist said. It is not uncommon. Dwelling on it will only make things worse. It's just a dream, it will go away."

He lay in beside me and gathered me into his arms.

"No, it won't, Sarah. Here it goes again. It won't go away. None of it makes sense. Just when I thought everything was coming together."

It was around that time the *Somnos* project came to light. Like everyone else I saw the press conference that evening on the news. Kevin Barret with that deadpan look on his face telling the nation about this project that sounded like something out of a fifties sci-fi novel: five comatose prisoners on the flat of their backs in Killary harbour exploring something which may or may not prove to be the future of penal incarceration across the EU—incredible. Listening to him that evening was one of those moments that has you turning to the person beside you and asking, Did he just say what I think he said—a penal experiment with coma patients? And Kevin delivered it all in that toneless drone of his like it was the most obvious thing in the world. It was a riveting performance. I've never had an interest in politics but even I could see that Kevin was impressive that evening. I've never seen a public official coming before the people so clued into his work; Kevin had all the angles covered. He started with a brief outline of the project's origins and then a close detailing of the binding legal and scientific protocols. Then he segued into the medical precedents, lobbing out those technical terms as if they were part of some new manifesto. He rounded off the whole thing with a brief itemising of the costings bill which was being drawn up by the Department of Finance. Forty-two minutes of droning monotone without once having to refer to notes or repeat an essential point. Someone has pointed out that in all the interviews he's given since he's not once contradicted a word of that original press conference. But of course the essential subtext of the whole performance was that this was not up for discussion; this was a *fait accompli*—there were no legal or constitutional barriers, everything was in order Kevin assured us. The only outstanding thing was an Irish volunteer.

As a piece of salesmanship it was masterful.[†]

The following day's editorials missed the point completely, spilled ink agonising over ethics and safety and failed to see the real motives behind the whole thing. Or so JJ informed me.

"They've missed the point," he said, smiling and tapping the paper. "Kevin has blinded them. PR firms will study this in years to come, a textbook example of misdirection—how to tell the truth and sidetrack people at the same time."

[†] Worries that the experiment would become a penal conduit which sped a criminal under-class straight from sentencing into a state sponsored oblivion were seized upon by many commentators. If coma were to become a sentencing option would there not be the likelihood that it would draw the bulk of its participants from the ranks of under-class offenders? Could any judiciary be trusted with such an option? Wasn't this a blatant attempt by the state to cull, however temporarily, a whole class of offenders and wash its hands of all educational and rehabilitative responsibilities? Were we now looking towards the day when the

"It sounds crazy, the whole thing."

"Even the timing was brilliant," JJ marvelled. "Nine o'clock at night, early enough to gather a few thoughts together but no time to sift through the info and reset today's editions with real analysis. That's why we have all this useless agonising about safety and ethics. Kevin handed that to them on a plate, that's why he spelled it out in such detail."

"But that is the real issue, talk about walking blind—who knows what might happen to those volunteers."

"It's a smokescreen, Sarah, all that information . . . It's a done deal also. By the time people grasp what's really at issue here those volunteers will be on the broad of their backs sucking three square meals a day through their IVs."

"So what is the issue?"

"This is a quid pro quo. Think about it. Stumbling over the Nice Treaty, shuffling our feet over tax harmonisation, environmental legislation on the long finger, neutrality, an economic policy looking towards Boston rather than Berlin . . . What's at stake here is not just the future of penal incarceration but our bona fides as good EU citizens."

---

ranks of hoodied recidivists would be thinned out so that a better class of white collar offender would have the run of our prison institutions. . . ? Furthermore, it was argued, that with no binding terms within the experiments constitution, the degree to which faith in its democratic draw was vested in a governing moral calculus was worrying, to say the least. Could it be relied upon to keep the whole thing honest? Was it not worrying that this very calculus was grounded in the same bloodless over-realm in which the project itself had its origins?

"And we need their approval that badly?"

"Kevin is looking at the bigger picture. This project will be carried out before the eyes of the world, a gallery of expectant nations looking on, fingers crossed that the whole thing comes up trumps and that souls can be racked and stacked in prison ICUs, atoning at half the price of five-star hotel accommodation."

"There'll be outcry."

"Only to begin with, some liberal hand-wringing and agonising but Kevin's betting on the people's short attention span and desire for a quiet life."

"I can't see it making economic sense—all the technology, the manpower, its ridiculous."[†]

JJ laughed and waved the paper. "I don't know about that; nothing is as ridiculous as the present system. The only prison system in Europe with more warders than prisoners, two-thirds of its entire budget spent on salaries and overtime, no rehab programmes . . . anything has to be an improvement on that. But it's not just about budgets, Sarah. It's about knowledge also—the meeting of minds, the exchange of ideas—the big flaw within the concept of punitive incarceration. Prisons are criminogenic and our prisons are institutes of higher learning. You go in knowing how to steal a Volkswagen Golf and come out knowing how to rip off a BMW. But you're not going to be able to

---

[†] Somewhere there's a formula justifying all this . . . Fixed as part of the greater national index in some ideational realm within the here and now, a place where abstracts like guilt and atonement are assigned certain values and reckoned as a percentage of all public spending . . . And this being an age of numeracy we've watched the coefficients become serial offenders, outstripping population growth and available resources,

learn much when you're out cold trying to raise a delta wave."

"That's as brutish a rationale as I've ever come across."

"That's why Kevin's appealed to our vanity: an opportunity to show that we have the courage and expertise to guide this cutting-edge experiment. What Kevin wants to show is that we've moved on from the days of the Celtic Tiger. We're not just a nation of mobile-phone salesmen or telesales spooks or production-line ops. We've left that potty training behind us—we're out there now with a shiny piece of R&D all our own. We have the brains, we have the funding, all we need is a lab rat."

"These are real people, JJ. Who knows what might happen to them."

"I don't know. Is a person in a coma a person? Is it meaningful to talk in any way about a subject with no consciousness?" He laid the paper on the table.

"Don't start that guff, JJ, splitting hairs."

"You're right; what's needed here are men of action not philosophers."

"Tough, that rules you out so. Anyway, you're not a criminal."

"That's just it. The Irish volunteer has to be an innocent, no criminal record needed—in fact, a criminal record will put you clean out of the running. They need a control,

---

gaining on that siren-ringing cut-off point where cost analysis has drawn a line and said this far and no further. Fast-forward from a time when the *lingua franca* of national well-being gladdened us as a stream of stats issuing from government departments and research bodies, we now find all indicators flatlining, a general refusal to respond to the old stimuli. The conclusions are obvious: the old options are exhausted.

an innocent in good health who establishes a baseline condition. An exemplar so to speak. Fair play to Kevin—even within a coma he's managed to stake out the high moral ground for the Paddy."

"All this enthusiasm, where has your guilt gone all of a sudden?—I've heard enough about it these past two years."

"I've told you before I'm not guilty of anything; I'm just guilty, that's all."

"And now you can walk away from it just like that."

"All I'm saying is . . . three months on the flat of your back, full bed and board . . ."

"Don't even think about it, JJ."

He looked into the distance. "My point exactly, Sarah, there is nothing to think about."

And I knew then he was going to go for it and nothing I or anyone else could say would stand in his way.

ANTHONY O'MALLEY

I picked the letter up inside the door and saw his name on it; then I saw the Department of Justice stamp in the right-hand corner. My first thought was what the hell has he been up to now?. . . As far as I could remember JJ had never received anything other than a polling card from the government. He was at the table, eating a bite of breakfast when I handed it to him. He read it at arm's length, chewing a piece of bread, then folded it back into its crease and handed it to me without a word or expression on his face.

I couldn't believe it.

"Tell me this is the wrong address, JJ," I said, a moment later. "The wrong man, the wrong house."

He just sat there looking at me with this blank look on his face.

I threw up my hands. "Mother of Jesus. Are you fucking crazy . . . ?"

We had it out hammer and tongs then, one of the worst rows we've ever had. I had thought that these kinds of arguments were behind us, that we had moved beyond them into some sort of man-to-man understanding of each other. But then this crops up, of all the frigging things.

Of course I lost the head straight off.

"Do you have any fucking idea what the hell you are letting yourself in for with this?"

Of course I was roaring now and knew even as I heard myself that if I kept it up this would be the end of the conversation. Keeping my wits about me was what was needed now—a clear head and a sharp wit. I had to meet him on his own ground if I was going to make any headway.

"Well?" I said, waving the letter in the air. "Well?"

He leaned back in his chair and massaged his temples. I could sense one of his speeches coming on. But he just shook his head.

"If you're going to start ranting and raving we're not going to get anywhere with this. Of course I don't know what I am letting myself in for. That's the nature of the whole thing."

"For the love of Christ, JJ, think about this . . ."

I spread the letter out on the table and took a step back from it. The government seal, the green harp at the top of the page—that was the bit I couldn't get over. How could an official document, a government document, land on a person's doorstep with news like this, news that might just as well have come from another world. Had everyone gone off their heads?

". . . JJ, let's consider this. You're only out of hospital a few months. You've got the all-clear and now you want to go and sign up for this fucking thing."

He said nothing, just sat there knowing full well that I would talk myself out if I went on long enough. And of course he was giving me every chance and, true to form, I took it.

"What the hell do you think you're going to do with yourself for those three months—count sheep?"†

He looked me square in the eye. "Nothing I say will make you understand this. I don't have the words for it myself much less anyone else." He drew his hand across his face. "These thoughts," he said after a pause, "these dreams, this constant mind-racing and mindrot . . . now this ghost. It just wears me down. A break from myself, that's what I need. Just to take myself off somewhere and forget myself for a while."

It made no sense to me; it made no sense to me then and it makes no sense to me now either. This idea of forgetting himself . . . someone as smart as JJ trying to forget himself . . . and after all he'd been through . . . There was something here that flummoxed me but I hadn't the turn of mind to put my finger on it. Keep to what you know I told myself—or at least what you think you know.

I pulled out a chair and sat down. I needed something solid under me.

"JJ, when people are down in themselves they don't go

---

† At 2:23 A.M. on the morning of the twenty-third of August a spectacular anomaly occurred across the transmitted EEGs of all five subjects. In a sudden leap beyond the phase and amplitude of their coma signatures each patient appeared to achieve a brief period of full consciousness. Staggered at three-second intervals the alpha waves of Luftig, Jorda, Perec and Callanan lasted a full seventeen seconds before full unconsciousness resumed. Trailing twelve seconds behind this serial

signing up for this sort of thing. People take up hobbies, they go on holidays, they do other things . . . But this . . ."
I stabbed a finger at the letter. "JJ, you've spent the whole of these last ten months recovering, trying to find your way back to yourself and now you want to do this. Throwing away all you've worked for—all we've worked for, I might add."

That surprised me—it was out of me before I could check it and I regretted it the moment the words left my mouth. This sense of having a claim over him just because of my part in his recovery . . . A mean sort of feeling you never know you have until someone threatens it. Of course he picked up on it straight away.

"Don't start that," he said. "This is not a question of ownership." He smoothed out the form and pushed it across the table to me. "Your signature, this is where your name goes. Next of kin." He drew his finger along the bottom of it.

If ever I had a serious mind to stand in his way then this is the moment when I should have done it. This is where I could have quit the room and put a stop to everything. But of course no more than JJ himself I could never walk away from an argument either. Sometimes I think this fondness for a scrap is one of those things

---

cluster JJ O'Malley registered a full ten-second alpha wave. Comparisons between the transmitted data and the secure data within the *Somnos* ICU revealed that the anomaly could only be the work of external hackers. An immediate investigation traced the signal to a cybernetic project within the MediaLab research institute in Dublin; sampled EEGs of a dog and four sheep had been spliced into the ongoing cursive of each patient's coma, the effect in this case being of

I've given him, this hunger to see every argument through to the last word, this wish to be the last man standing. I know that that's my way; is now and always has been. And then sometimes I think it's something we took from each other . . .

"My next of kin. You have to sign this release."

His tone of voice—it was like he was asking me to sign for a bill of goods and expected no problem, just sitting there with no expression on his face, the cup and plate on the table before him.

"And I suppose I'm the last to hear about this?"

"The only other one who knows is Sarah."

"And she's going along with this as well, this whole fucking—"

"—She's not thrilled but she's not ranting or raving either."

He motioned to the form once more, tapped his finger on it.

I shook my head.

He was calm, with the quiet look of a man who'd already won the argument. He was giving me the impression that I had slipped up somewhere along the way and that it was only a matter of him bringing me back through my own words and having him show me the flaw in them. But when

---

a pure-bred collie herding a small flock of black-faced mountain hoggets through the featureless topography of a five-man coma. Refusing to acknowledge the joke, a project spokesman drily confirmed that while telemetry would remain online all transmission would henceforth be secured within military-grade encryption codes. Proceedings to bring charges of virtual trespass against the hackers are still ongoing.

he spoke it was nothing like what I'd expected and it was probably the only other question I could have answered no to.

"Have I ever asked you for anything before?" he said.

KEVIN BARRET TD

The morning of the press conference he was standing at reception with a small bag at his feet and a bottle of water in his hands.

"JJ . . . you're on your own?"

"Kevin . . . yes, I thought it would be better to keep it simple. No reason to get anyone involved at this time."

"Yes, keep it simple." I motioned to the big man beside me. "JJ, this is Detective Sergeant Dermot Melia. He's my security but I'm handing him over to you for the next two days."

JJ held out his hand. "Security?"

"Just for these two days, you're public property now, JJ, we have to look after you. Let's sit down for a minute."

We moved to two armchairs inside the windows. The mid-morning crowds passed by outside. JJ stretched out his legs and drank from his bottle. He looked pale.

"Have you eaten? . . . You look a bit nervous."

"More tired than nervous . . . I hate that train journey, hate journeys of any sort."

"You'll have a few hours to yourself this afternoon. Try and get some sleep before we move out. Do you have a mobile?"

"No, I hate those as well."

"My God, I thought they were a fifth limb for your generation. Take this. There are two programmed numbers, mine and Dermot's. Dermot will be down here at reception if you need him. The number is purely back-up, just in case you get separated."

"It sounds like a military operation."

"Yes, that's exactly what it is. This is where it begins and it has to go by the numbers as they say, no screw-ups. Have you read the handout?"

"I should know my own biog by now."

"Just so you know what they know because that's where all their questions will come from. We're holding on to it till the last moment. They will be given it about half an hour before you make your entrance. Try and stick to the facts this evening—remember that you're in charge here. The trickiest moment will be when they ask about your motives."

"Don't worry I'll keep it simple: no philosophising or theorising, just the facts."

"Exactly. They'll know from your biog how smart you are and that's an invitation to debate, they'll try to trip you up. Don't give them an opening. Give them as little as possible in your best manners. Forty-five minutes, that's all it will come to, then we get you back here and you can be on your way home tomorrow."

"I have all these clothes with me, I'm not sure what to wear."

"Come as you are, keep it simple. Go and get some sleep now. I'll order some dinner and get it sent up to you. Remember, Dermot will be here if you need him."

"What time?"

Dermot handed him his bag. "Don't worry, I'll wake you up."

The thing about press conferences is that you try to anticip-ate two things: who the questions are going to come from and what specifically they are going to address. That way you make sure all the answers are stacked on your side of the table from the off. Of course you're never going to have all the angles covered but the more eventualities you cover the better the impression you make. We were the ones making the impression that evening and we had our home-work done.

When we arrived at the empty conference hall I got him to sit behind the table on his own. I took a seat in the center of the room and tried placing myself in the mind of those who would be seeing him for the first time. He was wearing his blue jeans and a long-sleeved T-shirt, looking taller and thinner than he really was; with his height and dark looks I knew he would physically dominate the table. Those journalists were going to meet a young man with the sort of features and cheekbones you see in those glossy scent advertisements, the type of face the new Ireland doesn't wonder at any more.[†]

"How does it feel up there?"

He spread his hands flat on the table and looked around

[†] Those vectors which have converged here—epidemiological, political, economic . . . detonating on impact, cluttering the air with fragments should not occlude the fact that when the smoke clears and the light coalesces we are back in the neuro-ICU looking at five men submerged in the deep end of the Glasgow Coma Scale, sunk beneath

him. "I'm looking forward to it, it will be a relief to get this out in the open and have the whole thing under way. The sooner the better."

"I'll be there on your left. Have you your wits about you?"

He nodded. "So long as I'm not sitting on them."

He didn't show any nerves beside me that evening. Halfway through my opening statement he rolled the sleeves of his T-shirt up to his elbows—the country lad breaking out in him. For one moment I thought he might spit in the palms of his hands and say something like, "OK, lads, let's get down to work."

My opening statement covered once more the origins and rationale behind the project. Then a short intro into JJ himself. This was just a ploy to give him time to get his bearings, a soft entry into the whole thing. When I finished I turned to him and asked him if there was anything he wanted to add. As we'd planned he just shook his head and I opened the discussion to the floor. A security correspondent put his hand up and identified himself.

"Good evening, JJ, I wonder could we have some word from you as to why you wanted to volunteer for this project. I wonder if you could say something about that."

JJ nodded and leaned out on his elbows. He spoke quietly, without hesitation. It must have been impressive hearing him for the first time.

"I've given my reasons in my application, I think you

---

the pupillary response and the gag reflex . . . When the smoke drifts away, and insofar as these things are ever clear to us, we might see how near or far this altarpiece is from being another of those blurred nexus of the good, the true and the beautiful.

have that there in front of you . . . As it says, I want to go to sleep, to take my mind off my mind. These last couple of years haven't been a happy time for me. I want to go to sleep so that I can get a rest from myself and my thoughts. It is a fairly simple idea—all I want to do is lie down and get some sleep."

"Have you any fears?—the whole project seems risky to put it mildly."

"I'm more curious than afraid. Of course there is a degree of fear; I would worry about myself or anyone else if they were not afraid going into something like this. But at this moment I have to say my curiosity outweighs my fears."

"Have you any worries for your health?"

"No, this project has been researched. When it's got to the point where people are being used as guinea pigs then you have to presume that all the angles have been covered. Of course anything can happen in something like this but in answer to your question, no, I have no worries."

Everything was going smoothly up to this, everything running to predictions. The coaching we put him through was standing to him. But then, as we'd predicted, a question about his background. It came from one of the red-top journalists.

"JJ, your background, an adopted child coming from a single-parent family—do you think that has anything to do with your decision to volunteer for this?"

It didn't faze him. He moved into it without hesitation.

"The reasons for my decision are laid down in my application and they have nothing to do with my background. Yes, I am an adopted child from a single-parent family and in that I consider myself very lucky. All children are born but I was not only born I was chosen also. That makes me feel very special. Nothing in my life has made me feel I have lacked for anything, least of all love. I have no grievance or issues with being an adopted child. That is too easy, too cry-baby."

The combative edge in his voice was noted the next day in the newspapers. Before the journalist could come back for a second bite I signalled to another raised hand.

"What's been the reaction of your father to your volunteering?"

"His reaction was that of any loving parent. As you can imagine he is more than a little worried. But we sat down together and talked it through. I can't say he's happy about it but it is my wish and he respects that."

"When did he first hear about this?"

"The day I was shortlisted. I told him that morning."

We were alone in the hall after the journalists filed out. JJ stood up clutching the plastic bottle of water. I would never meet him again without one of those bottles in his hands, a kind of security blanket, a small shield against the world.

"That went fine," I said. "You did well."

"I'm going back to the hotel," he said. "I need to make a few calls."

"You'll watch the nine o'clock news?"

"No—I can wait for tomorrow's reviews."

"Have you any plans for tonight? Now that you're in the big smoke is there anything you want to do?"

"No, I'm going to stick to my room. I'll probably raid the minibar and watch some TV."

"Good, you look like you could do with some sleep."

The following morning this tall fella with shades and a red bandanna on his head walked up to me at reception and stood in front of me. Out the corner of my eye I saw Dermot by the lift door looking blankly at me. The tall fella in front of me wasn't saying anything or moving and for a moment I thought I had wandered into some sort of a stand-off. After a long moment he pulled off the shades and grinned.

"Will this throw them for a few hours?"

"It threw me," I said. "Yes, for a few hours but no more."

"I saw the papers after breakfast so I went out and got sheared. The hairdresser wouldn't take any money but I signed and dated a ziplock bag before I left."

"She's going to sell you off one snip at a time in a month.† If you don't fancy the train Dermot can drive you home."

He shook his head. "No, let's keep it simple while we can. Sarah is coming to get me at the station."

"Whatever you say. *Thoughtful and articulate, wearing his genius IQ up front. An unlikely candidate for such an*

---

† Listed on ebay.co.uk on the seventeenth of July this item drew a steady stream of bids to its online auction. Ten minutes before the close of its seven-day listing a bid of €1,000 secured the trophy for Krayfeld Records in Oslo, a specialist music store already in possession of an extensive collection of memorabilia from the death-metal wars of the early nineties. An interview with the owner Stein Ommund Svendsen said the hair would be exhibited above the reissues of Luftig's two-CD back catalogue.

JJ becoming his own memorabilia is a further example of what one commentator has termed the "metastasisation of the project beyond

adventure. You've made an impression, JJ, the photos looked well."

"So the hairdresser said. *The kind of young man any mother would be glad to see her daughter bringing home.* I hope Sarah's parents read that."

"That'll play for a few days. Brace yourself for the claw-back though."

"That's the bit that worries me."

"That's fame for you." I handed him a red folder. "Have a read of this on the train. It's the biogs of the other subjects."

"Have you met any of them?"

"No, nor have they met each other. You will meet together in Castelrea Prison two weeks from now. You will be brought together for the first time for the induction sessions. That will take a week—a detox session, the last medical checks and psychological checks. Your job from now till then will be to look after yourself. No injuries or mad drinking sessions. And that girlfriend of yours—Sarah—I'd get my fill of her before I leave if I were you . . . it could be a long three months."

"Yes."

Dermot ran him to the train. I let them go alone, my

---

its scientific parameters into an info-and-memento disposal phenom-enon. However, it is now not enough that we see and hear these things, some of us have to possess them as well; only that we feel we can not believe." The same commentator noted that this transaction echoed somewhat the circumstances of JJ's adoption from the orphanage.

A follow-up piece in a national tabloid showed the hairdresser, Emily Rynne, twenty-four, smiling and displaying her cheque outside the hair salon. The money, she said, would go towards her upcoming hen party in Ibiza.

presence would only draw attention to him, defeating the purpose of the haircut. He phoned me later that evening to tell me that journalists were already outside his house but he had refused as politely as he could to say anything.

GERARD FALLON

You could feel the town bracing itself the night JJ gave that press conference. The pubs were full and of course there was only one topic of conversation on the agenda. To say that people were stunned would be putting it mildly. What the hell was he thinking of? What did he hope to gain from it? The consensus was that no one in his right mind would put himself forward for such a job. Of course someone said this was exactly the point—JJ was not in his right mind, hadn't he spent a full month in the ceilidh house not so long ago? How had this ever escaped the people who were supposed to be screening those volunteers? Listening to all the talk it struck me that if JJ thought he was going to get any admiration for what he was doing he was going to be sorely mistaken. Even in those first hours after the press conference you could sense the town raising its guard. They knew what was coming. This town would now be held up to scrutiny in a way it had not earned or prepared itself for. It's not the kind of attention any place wants drawing on itself. No one was going to thank him for it.

I was glad he wasn't around that night.

I got a call from him the following morning, around ten

o'clock. He sounded calm, like a man with a good night's sleep behind him.

"Well, JJ, that's some pyjama party you've signed up for."

"So I believe. I'm calling from Dublin, Ger, I'm coming down on the evening train. The reason I'm calling you . . . you saw the press conference last night?"

"The whole country saw it. You came across very well. Confident and resolute, the square-jawed young man with the right stuff."

"Good. I'm just putting you on your guard here. Sooner rather than later the press is going to start asking more questions. That stuff at the press conference was just the bare bones, they're going to come looking for more. I just wanted you to be aware of that. I've rung around a few other people."

There was a different tone in his voice then, a note I'd never heard before. He was low-key, tentative—moods I didn't readily associate with him. It took me a moment to figure it out: JJ was on the defensive. For the first time in all my years of knowing him he was on the back foot about one of his ideas, anxious for others and the consequences of what he was doing. Was he looking for reassurance? I wondered.

"Fair enough, JJ," I said. "I haven't seen or heard from anyone yet but as you say it's probably only a matter of time. I haven't been up town this morning yet so I don't know who's around." There was a pause on the other end of the line but I could hear his thoughts. "Don't worry, you're one of our own. We'll talk you up."

He laughed. "Thanks. I don't like putting you in this position but there's no way out of it. You know yourself that if certain things got out how they can be made to look. A bad situation could be made to look a lot worse."

"No worries. How are things besides? You looked confident on the box. Are you nervous?"

"I feel fine. Today's reviews are pretty much what we expected: curiosity and bewilderment. Things will get critical from now on."

"I suppose you've answered this more than once already but do you know what you're doing?"

He laughed again, the kind of laugh he kept for those moments in our discussions when he was about to deliver some telling point. "No," he said, "I don't know what I'm doing. I'm not so sure either whether knowing would be a good thing. What I do know is that I want to go through with it. I'll probably call you in the next few days. I have two weeks to myself before this thing starts."

"Make sure you call round before you go away."

"I will. Many thanks, Ger."

"Sound."

I took a walk out after that phone call just to see if indeed the world's press had descended on our little town. As far as I could see there was no one around, just the same quiet street you'd expect at that hour of the morning. When I stepped into Kelly's for the paper JJ's face was spread over every front page on the shelf. The same colour photo in each one as if JJ had only presented this one glimpse of himself for examination. It showed him seated behind the table looking straight into the camera, no expression on his face. His left hand was outstretched on the table before him, clutching that plastic bottle of water. If I'm not mistaken a cropped version of this photo is the standard portrait of JJ you now see everywhere.

Eddie took the money from me. "We know he has brains but do you think has he any sense?"

"It's an adventure, Eddie, that's what young men go for."

"He's brave though, I'll give him that." Walter Crayn came in behind me and picked up the *Irish Times*. "Three months' room and board with no worries . . . there could be worse ways of spending a wet summer."

Eddie opened a tabloid on the counter. "He was always a bit odd, the same JJ. He'd come in here some mornings with his head in the clouds; it was like drawing teeth getting talk out of him. You'd wish him luck though. That's all I can say."

"Twenty purple as well, Eddie," Walter said. "Let's hope luck has nothing to do with it. I suppose we'll be going out to the Killary from now on to keep an eye on him."

That conversation drew me up. My reading of it was that the disbelief and bewilderment of the previous night had given way to a cautious support. A night's sleep had allowed us to order our thoughts and put aside whatever reservations we had in our hearts. He'd made his decision and being one of our own we would support him whatever way we could. We weren't without doubts or indeed cynicism but we would stand behind him. Walking out of the shop that morning I felt good for him, more confident.

I was sitting down to a pile of exam papers when I got the first call: a feature writer from the *Irish Times*. He was looking for what he called background colour, anything that might help the public get a clearer view of our new hero, as he put it. How long had I known him and what kind of student had he been? What were his interests, how did I think the town would react to one of their young men volunteering for such a project?

My speech was ready. JJ's call had prompted me to put a few thoughts together. I was as bland as I could be without giving offence.

"I've known the lad since he was thirteen years old. He was a pupil here in the local school and teachers and pupils alike were very fond of him. He made friends with everyone during those years, made friends and kept them."

"What was he like as a pupil? Seemingly he was very bright."

"Yes, that's well known, very gifted. JJ has an IQ which allows him to turn his mind to anything. It was obvious to everyone who taught him that he was an exceptional young man."

"Did you think he ever suffered for his intelligence?"

"No, certainly not to a degree that will allow for any cheap theorising."

"What I'm getting at is do you think his intelligence and the fact that he was adopted left him with some want in his heart which he might hope this project would fulfil?"

"Nothing I know about JJ leads me to believe that there is a want in his heart or his head or any other place. He is

182

a questing soul, there's no doubt about that, but I'm firmly
of the belief that this is because of an unusually sharp mind,
not the result of some existential malaise as you might put
it. You have to remember JJ is read beyond his years. He
could put any of his teachers to shame in any discussion.
Always questioning, always looking for answers." I drew
myself up and tried to change tack. "This is beginning to
sound like an obituary; I hope it's not going to come across
like that tomorrow."

"No, but as I say there is a real shortage of background
detail on him. Always looking for answers you say. How do
you think JJ imagines a three-month coma will provide any
answers?"

"I wouldn't presume to know what's on JJ's mind nor
should anyone else either. All you need to know is that he
is a young man any teacher would be proud of. JJ has a lot
of goodwill coming to him. Let's hope he comes through this
unharmed and that he can get on with his life."

"Are you worried about him?"

"As JJ himself has said, anyone in their right mind would
have worries."

That interview was quoted verbatim the following day,
padding out a ream of pop psychology and low-grade sociology.
The most accurate part of it was the headline, a four-word
phrase which sounded like the first line of a lonely heart's
ad: *Restless Mind Seeks Rest.*

It wouldn't be the first time this village had someone who
flirted with his own death like this.

If you go out this road about two miles and turn left

after the sign for Conlon's timber yard you'll see this big hall in off the road on your left. The roof is stripped away now, the whole thing falling in on itself.[†] You wouldn't think to look at it but back in the seventies this was one of the most hopping dance halls in the county. In 1972 a Cork man by the name of Considine—Mick Considine I think, a P&T worker—made an attempt on the world record for being buried alive in that dance hall. Raising money he was for some sort of sheltered housing project below in Cork . . . A section of the floor was lifted up and Considine was lowered down in a coffin. They timbered up the hole and a slab of concrete was poured over him. A small headstone and a limestone border finished off the whole thing. That evening while the band played we literally danced on his grave into the early hours of the morning. Five days was all he lasted. An attack of claustrophobia nearly choked him and it was only by the skin of his teeth that he was broken out by two local lads with a pair of twelve-pound hammers.

I'd forgotten that story until someone drew it down the night of JJ's press conference. More than one person has mentioned it to me since.

[†] There's this downturn across the land, all indicators flatlining across charts and screens, a blank refusal to respond to the old stimuli. Somehow the coma has leaked out through the security perimeter, found its way into the ambience of the nation and once more become the national idiom. Of course the causal sequence may be the other way round but one way or another we have thrown in our lot and gone native in it, remembering once more a way of being that is second nature to us. And while no one can finger the exact time or place where the rot set in, the place where bad went to worse, there

KEVIN BARRET TD

They were flown in separately, the helicopters touching down in the exercise yard at half-hour intervals. After they were billeted in their separate chalets I went to the mess hall to greet them. My hope was that they'd be sitting around in a comradely huddle talking together, taking their first steps towards bonding as a team. Some hope. When I entered the hall Didac and Emile and JJ were gathered at one end of the longest table with their backs to me; Haakan and Jimmy Callanan were sitting beneath them locked in a ferocious arm wrestle. You didn't need to do much looking to see who had the upper hand . . . Jimmy was breathing hard, leaning into his right shoulder, a vein throbbing along his jawbone. As I approached his left hand shot out and grabbed the end of the table. Luftig looked up at me and then turned away with blank disinterest. Then, baring his teeth, he suddenly drove Jimmy's arm down on to the table with a brutal heave, toppling the Scotsman from his chair on to the floor. A guffaw broke over the table. Emile Perec reached out and held up

is general agreement that there has been this general shift, not of mass but of minds and energy. Every analysis points to exhaustion and fatigue, some essential component in the engine itself worn out, pleading for time out, an extended rest period where it can draw its breath and gather its strength . . .

the Swede's hand. *Le champion*, he yelled, *le champion du monde*. That done, the five of them split up and moved off to separate seats, as far away from each other as the confines of the hall would allow. Luftig immediately wired himself into his Discman and Perec opened up a comic on the table and buried his head in it.

It wasn't the start I'd anticipated. Straight off I saw we had a de facto leader and his fool in our midst; a hierarchy of sorts had already asserted itself. Any hope of them coming together in an atmosphere of respect and camaraderie was going be disappointed. It was obvious they were going to keep their distance from each other for as long as they deemed it necessary. If not outright contempt for each other the impression they gave was one of studied indifference. And a captive audience they might well be but they were determined to prove difficult.

It was not a time for speechifying. I said a few words of welcome, called out their names, commended them on their bravery and assured them that whatever the scientific aims of the project nothing would compromise their health and safety. I wished them well and told them that all the educational and recreational facilities of the prison were available to them. If they were grateful they did a good job of keeping it to themselves. JJ was the only one who showed any interest in what I had to say but I knew better than to believe it was anything other than politeness.

Looking at them then I mentally scrapped one of the PR ploys we had scheduled for later that week. We had hoped to bring them before the public in a final televised press conference from inside the prison. It would be the final part of our hearts-and-minds operation—five articulate speakers coming before the nation with a suitable sense of historic opportunity about them. All objections would wilt in the face of such humility and square-jawed resoluteness. At least that had been the idea. But one look at those sullen expressions and the likelihood of them blanking an assembly of political correspondents made me think better of it.

If any part of the project was badly managed it was this induction week. The decision to house them in separate chalets within the prison was a mistake. It failed to draw them together—in fact, it did nothing but make them all the more resolute in their separateness. From the outset they made it known that they wanted nothing to do with each other. They ate separately, exercised separately and sat in opposite corners of the reading room. Not once during the entire week did anyone witness a pair of them in conversation with each other. In fact, it became clear that they would do everything in their power and within the confines of the prison to keep out of each other's way. Marking out their separate space and identities became each man's individual project for that week. It was something I hadn't foreseen, a variable I hadn't reckoned on and it made me anxious.

Jane Evers, the prison psychologist, spelled it out for me. Her read on the situation was that they should not be forced to bond if they did not want to. Within the aims and protocols of the experiment there was no need or reason why they should. This was not a team-building exercise they were limbering up for nor was it some type of Special Forces mission; these models did not obtain. In their separate comas they would have no need of each other, they would not be reliant on each other for anything like skills, logistical or moral support. They would endure alone and isolated and it was obvious they had resolved to start as they were going to finish. Furthermore, she warned, they were likely to react negatively to any ploy which might seek to draw them together. A reasoned understanding of what they were undertaking should be assumed and must not be offended by dressing up the project as anything other than what it really was. This final individuation should be respected; it was their time to themselves. If they wanted this to change then it was for them to say so; if they didn't then nothing was lost bar an atmosphere of camaraderie.

It made sense but it still left a worry. As something we hadn't foreseen it hinted at God knows how many other things lay down the road to jump out at us. Confined within the prison and mercifully out of the public gaze it was of no real consequence but I didn't want the project proceeding on this ad hoc basis. Smoothness and certainty and openness—these were our watchwords.

At the end of the second day I called a meeting of all the advisers on secondment to the project to run through the whole thing from bow to stern.

This was the most fretful week of the entire project—everything afterwards was calmness itself compared to the anxiety of those few days. Our biggest problem was still trying to get public opinion onside, assuaging the fears of those letter writers and commentators who were still harping on the ethical difficulties of the project. By then, however, there was an unmistakable air of futility about the whole debate. The project was now under way and all these objections and scruples were only so much hot air. Nevertheless, my time was taken up with media appearances, debates, radio phone-ins . . . repeating assurances, rebutting objections, putting backspin on all the hostile articles and editorials which were still appearing. The Taoiseach himself spoke once on the subject. On the steps of the government jet, his stance was statesmanlike. A master of the public utterance he confined himself to a few bland assurances, emollient words, nothing which might give hostages to fortune. Then with a wave of his hand to the assembled press he turned his back and was gone. As I knew from the beginning of this whole thing I was on my own. It would make or break whatever political career lay ahead of me.

We were lucky with our timing though. As the Dáil had risen for summer recess we didn't have to cope with an organised attack from the opposition. Those few opposition spokesmen who did come out to speak on the subject gave such hapless performances it was obvious their protests were only a matter of form; their voices carried no conviction and they were easily countered. Appealing to the nation's scruples was a smokescreen, covering the fact that they themselves were largely in agreement with the project; a full year scoring easy points week in week out in debates on the prison crisis but offering no credible alternative had left them without leverage. Finally, when it was revealed that my opposite number's name was on one of the very first memorandums discussing the project at EU level, the ground was decisively cut from under them.

In one sense all those media appearances took my mind off the fact that actually there was very little I could do from now on. A rationale was in place and all negotiations were over; the machines were waiting to be plugged in, contracts had been filed and the principal roles had been assigned. We were now in clock-watching mode, waiting for the curtain to rise.

For security reasons I wanted to keep the exact commencement date a secret; justice department officials wouldn't hear of it. Openness and transparency they said, everything had to be above board and, more importantly, had to be seen to be above board. The public had to feel from the beginning that they were having as near as dammit complete access to the project; this was a public event. Secrecy and duplicity were to be avoided at all costs. Moreover, it was made known to me early on that press coverage of the start-up would be extensive. Sky News had negotiated exclusive rights for a live relay from inside the prison, specifically the moment when the volunteers assembled in the yard and moved out in convoy. Again I objected. It presented not just a security risk but a risk of real embarrassment. The convoy would be televised—who knew what protests or obstacles might materialise along the way. I urged a decoy—an empty convoy wending its way along the N60 towards the Killary drawing a press convoy in its wake while the volunteers were transported overhead in a Sea King helicopter. The ruse could be sold afterwards as a security measure and, I advised, such forward thinking would reflect well our anxiety to safeguard the volunteers. It took time and much back-room haggling but in the end department officials sat down and rejigged the terms of the transmission with Sky News.

We were conscious now that the whole thing was more theatre than politics. Even at this preliminary stage the project itself seemed the still point at the heart of a massive media event.[†] And because of that I wanted the whole thing shorn of as much colour and detail as possible. The volunteers for instance would wear their own clothes. Someone had suggested they might wear a one-piece uniform in the manner of NASA astronauts. This, it was thought, would be in keeping with the pioneering nature of the project. The volunteers put their foot down and I supported them. The less visual signatures this whole thing had the better. Of course we had no way at the time of foreseeing Luftig's stunt with the T-shirt; when that furore broke over us we had more than a little explaining to do. When he walked out into the exercise yard wearing jeans and leather jacket none of us suspected a thing.

Seeing the press posse haring down the N60 after the empty convoy gave us our only laugh of the day. When they were

---

[†] Whether or not the *Somnos* project had its precedent in those reality-TV incarcerations which bulked so large in the programming schedules of a couple of years ago is still a matter of debate. Theorists point out that the comatose condition of the subjects is the ultimate refinement of the witless compliance of all those contestants who never once sought to subvert the terms of their confinement from within. TV critics noted that those baseline dramas—tantrums, sulks, hissy fits and petty mind games—which intrigued so many viewers in the original

out of sight we led the volunteers from the mess hall and got them into the helicopter. Counting the pilot and co-pilot there were nine people on board. John Tierney, governor of Castlerea Prison, and myself were the only two civvies. This was a calculated risk. There was no way of knowing how the volunteers would react in these final minutes. Who knew what kind of panic might set in? Lifting off I saw John clasping his hand to his breast pocket—a final check to see that the syringes of sedatives were safely stowed.

It was a quiet first few minutes; you could feel the tension in the volunteers. They were leaning back with their eyes closed. As usual Haakan was wired up to his Discman, this grating thump coming from it. Emile was stuck in his comic and JJ was halfway down his bottle of water. Not for the first time I wished I had some words or speech ready and not for the first time I found myself without two words in my head. Thankfully Emile took his role as clown seriously. Without warning he lifted his head out of his comic and burst into song . . .

> Frère Jacques, Frère Jacques,
> Dormez-vous? Dormez-vous?
> Sonnez les matines,

---

versions had now been flatlined to a series of minimal cues and responses, decipherable only to a specialist audience. However, the fact that we do not know what we are watching nor how to interpret what it is we are watching is now apparently no obstacle to our watching.

In parallel with this analysis ran an especially paranoid theory—that the whole project was a trial run towards a partnership between media corporations and state penal systems. The privatisation of state

sonnez les matines,
Ding dang dong,
ding dang dong.

The other lads looked at each other and took up the chorus,
bawling it out with smiles and laughter till myself and John
were forced to join in. That song might be a lullaby but the
version I heard that day sounded more like a battle hymn
than anything you'd sing over a child. But it was obvious
what was happening; this was the moment of bonding delayed
to the moment of absolute necessity. They were looking round
at each other, brothers in arms now, cautious smiles on their
faces. JJ followed this up with "Hush Little Baby Don't You
Cry" and those of us who knew it took it up. That too was
longer and louder than I've ever remembered. A few more
songs then and when I looked out we were flying low, coming
up through the fjord. The decoy was pulling on to the cor-
doned pier side between the thronged press and onlookers.
We circled overhead a minute or so to give the crowd time
to settle and then put down on the opposite side of the pier
within a second cordon. We had the volunteers on the edge
of the slipway and inside the barriers before the crowd
twigged what was happening. They moved towards us and

---

prisons along American lines had been ongoing in Austria, France and
Britain since the mid-nineties and was now increasingly viewed as an opportunity to offload an exchequer expense on to the private sector . . .
However fanciful this theory may be, it would gain renewed currency
in the months after the *Somnos* project when the Italian media corpo-
ration Fininvest successfully tabled a bid for a prison franchise in its
home city of Milan.

of course, seeing his opportunity, this was the moment when Luftig took off his jacket and scandalised a nation. John Tierney made a move towards him but I pulled him back. Too late, I said. Let it go. They were at the end of the slipway before the press caught up with us, cameramen and reporters elbowing their way through the crowd, too late now to get any parting words from the volunteers. From the moment of touchdown to the moment they stepped into the dinghies, I'd say less than a minute. That above anything gave the whole thing its air of sudden anticlimax. Another minute and they were out in the middle of the fjord churning up a white wake behind them. Afterwards, of course, there was that criticism that we'd sent them on their way without any sort of ecumenical blessing, no words of spiritual fortitude, no sprinkling of holy water on their heads. We'd decided against it; a survey among them had established that all five of them, to a man, were faithless.

SARAH NEVIN

Cool is the new grace JJ used to say, the new electedness. You either have it or you don't, you can't buy it and there's no way of earning it. I thought of that this morning when my radio alarm went off and the first thing I heard was "Sound Sleep" . . . [†]

So what to wear today? Style mags don't cover these occasions. Like everyone else I have one of those T-shirts with his EEG graphic on the front. I bought it in the first weeks of the project before all those images were hemmed in by copyright law. Even now though you can't walk down any street without seeing it spread across someone's chest. Only yesterday I saw someone wearing *I Want To Take My Mind Off My Mind* on a cheap knock-off. It was only a matter of time I suppose before wilful mindlessness became the season's Zeitgeist.

Sitting on the side of the bed this morning it came to me

[†] An ambient chill-out groove, all synth washes and secular chants laid down over a systolic baseline; "Sound Sleep" became that summer's soundtrack. JJ's spoken-word lyric, sampled and edited from his one and only press conference, provided that summer's tautologous catch cry—*sleep never sleeps*. DJ Sandman's four-minute track went platinum across Europe and the bass hook—a looped précis of JJ's ditonal heartbeat—became the most downloaded ring tone for mobile-phone users . . .

that I've spent these last three months looking back at our time together. That surprised me. How is it possible to carry on day after day in a relationship and still have no clue just how much your life and soul is tied up in that someone else? There on the side of the bed was the first time I had any real idea of just how much I love him. And that surprised me too. In spite of all we've been through together, all the tragedies and injuries and arguments, all our days together seem to me to have been days of light and fun. There was never any talk of love or commitment between us, never any big avowals. We were together and that's all there was to it. Never once can I remember JJ telling me he loved me and for my part, if anyone had asked me did I love him, I would, more likely than not, have been stuck for an answer. We took each other so much for granted and that seems to me now no bad thing.

It's one thing me taking him for granted but the rest of the world doing the same . . . that's something that spooks me. That's my right, it's how we were, but it doesn't give the rest of the world the same right. These past few months, seeing him referenced all over the place like some hero or prophet has made me realise just how easy it is to reduce someone to a T-shirt slogan or a media profile. In spite of his presence all over the place people have forgotten JJ—the flesh-and-blood person has disappeared from view. In spite of all the words and images—or maybe because of them—JJ has faded away. But he's not some T-shirt slogan or discussion topic. He's more than that. He is someone beautiful and awkward, a son and lover, someone who is too smart for his own good but not smart enough to see that. People need reminding and that's why I'm telling you all this. Other people's motives I can't speak of but I know what I want; I want him to come back to himself, I want him to be here to meet himself when he walks off that boat and if talking him into the hearts and minds of people is what it takes then that's what I have to do. He told me once that death is no barrier to injury—another of those fancy paradoxes he was so fond of. He pointed out that when a person dies their identity lives on after them in all the things they leave behind, all the good and bad they've done, all the influences they've had. He didn't know how right he was but he didn't know either how someone can be traduced and misrepresented or, worse, turned into their own ghost, this alien presence. Of course were he to hear me now he'd throw his eyes up to heaven and feign a weakness. He once said that just because you can go on at length it doesn't mean you have something to say, it doesn't mean you have a story to tell; just because you've been unlucky or short-changed or fucked over or fallen heavily on the thorns of life—that's no justification. I beg to differ; sometimes we need others to speak on our behalf. JJ is smart, smarter than I'll ever be. I don't have his brains but I don't have his paranoia either. I can't see signs or make the connections he can—my world isn't shaped like that and I wouldn't want it shaped like that. It doesn't revolve around me and that's OK; I wouldn't want his sort of faith. So I'm not a character witness or a cheerleader—I'm just someone who cares. I don't want miracles, I'm not even interested in change. The old JJ is fine by me, I can cope with that. All

I want is that he should wake up to himself and pick up where he left off, pick up what it was he left off.

I woke up all nerves this morning, all twitchy and eager. I spent a few hours mooning around the house, listening to the radio in the kitchen. Of course the whole *Somnos* thing dominated the talk shows and phone-ins. Someone used the phrase "cognitive deficit" so I switched it off and went back upstairs to dress . . . So what does a girl wear to the resurrection? Do I go with the casual look or make a more formal effort? I want to strike the right note, classy not assy. After a few twirls in front of the mirror I decided on these trousers and this shirt—something between cool chick and cailín gleoite. Looking at my face I decided to tie my hair back; you wouldn't believe how much agonising went into so little.

And that's it. I've said all I've wanted to say, I'm ready now. So if you'll excuse me, it is getting near the time and I have to go . . . ‡

‡ . . . because on this day, the ninth of October, feast of St Denis, the patron saint of headaches, JJ O'Malley and his four companions emerge into the light, into the converged lenses of the world's press. Among those waiting for him are his father and lover, his teacher and neighbour and, standing at a politic remove but still in shot, his public representative.

They come up the slipway together, side by side, no precedence discernible between them now. Their stiff gait, the result of muscular atrophy and residual acid in their joints, lends the short walk a processional, almost liturgical air. For future reference we note that this season's well-dressed revenant is wearing a silver thermal cloak thrown casually over boots and T-shirt, accessorised with woollen cap pulled low over the forehead and wraparound shades shielding those sensitive retinas. But in the grey light it is difficult to distinguish one from the other. Their pallor and raiment, their sunken cheeks . . . something in their ordeal has reduced them to a sameness. And this is no time for confusion. This is where our onlookers need their wits about them. These subjects can be recovered, each to their separate selves, but they need these witnesses to differentiate . . . Flick back through the declensions of their IDs, through the oral testimony and documentation, the forensics and circumstantial evidence, the tracings and printouts, the photographs in the ID laminates; flick back and gain piece by piece on that dawning instant when each one stands clear and apart . . . But our witnesses are not as sure of themselves as we'd like and the flaw of reverse engineering defeats them at the conclusion. Incredibly though and stiff and all as he is, JJ is one step ahead of them. Seeing her face in the crowd triggers the causal stream of skin-to-synapse linkage throughout his central nervous system, blooming less than a heartbeat later in his hippocampus—the breathless recovery of her in him. In spite of appearances he has remained mindful of her, he has borne her in mind. His facial muscles broaden out beyond the blank stare of his media portraits. Then his voice sounds, dusty and faint from underuse but still up to the task of speaking for itself:

"Yes," he says, "I thought it was you."

All this in the nth year of what is still termed without irony the Age of Restored Salvation . . .

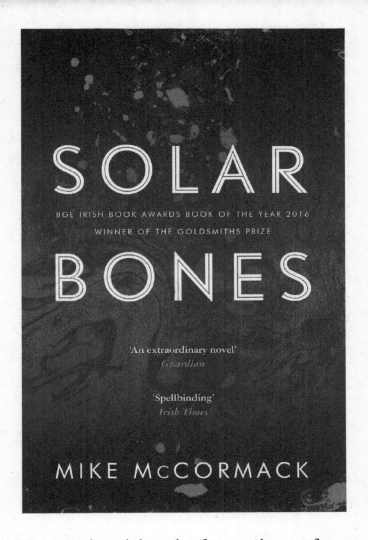

SOLAR

BGE IRISH BOOK AWARDS BOOK OF THE YEAR 2016
WINNER OF THE GOLDSMITHS PRIZE

BONES

'An extraordinary novel'
Guardian

'Spellbinding'
Irish Times

MIKE McCORMACK

'Hauntingly sad, but also frequently very funny
– Proust reconfigured by Flann O'Brien'
Literary Review

CANON‖GATE

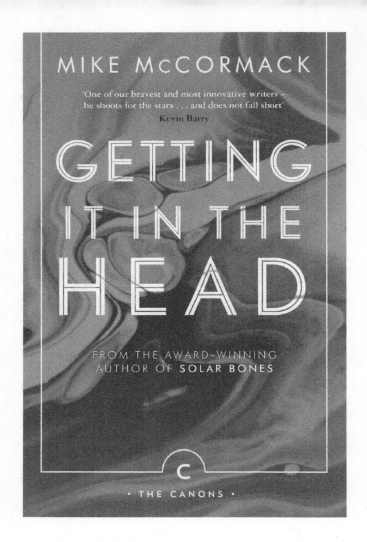

MIKE McCORMACK

'One of our bravest and most innovative writers –
he shoots for the stars . . . and does not fall short'
Kevin Barry

GETTING
IT IN THE
HEAD

FROM THE AWARD-WINNING
AUTHOR OF **SOLAR BONES**

· THE CANONS ·

'Funny, fantastical tales that trample
on the toes of the twentieth century itself'
New York Times

CANON▌GATE